A PICKLEBALL POISON

Dangerous Pastimes Series Book Three

Violetta Armour

By

Violetta Armour

- keep playing this awesome game - it will keep you young! But stay out of the kitchen ☺

Published by Gordian Books, an imprint of Winged Publications

ISBN: 978-1-952661-88-4

***Dedication**: To all my Arizona Pickleball Peeps in Sun Lakes, Evil League Ladies from Pecos Park, and Munds Park where I first learned to play and love the game.*

Quotes at beginning of chapters are taken from *Smart Pickleball, The Pickleball Guru's Guide,* with permission of author, Prem Carnot.

Special thanks to: Beta readers Chris Koski and Teri Dye. To Roberta Jennings and Tracy Thornock for editorial review and guidance. To Yvonne Brooks for her poker expertise and to Pharmacist, Dr. Dan Boatwright for information on the Prescription Drug Monitoring Program.

Epigraphs

"And now here is my secret, a very simple secret: It is only with the heart that one can see rightly; what is essential is invisible to the eye."
— Antoine de Saint-Exupéry, *The Little Prince*

A day well-lived or a game well-played is one in which you have consciously given the best version of yourself, no matter what that is.

The goal of this journey is to fine-tune your mindset to get the most out of your game and your life — and have fun along the way.

— *Pickleball and the Art of Living*, by Mike Brandon

AUTHOR NOTE:

It is no wonder that Pickleball is the fastest growing sport in America. The benefits are many. A game for all ages and especially seniors. I became addicted to the game many years ago and soon discovered that in addition to getting great exercise, it was a wonderful way to meet new people. Also that sitting on the sidelines or bleachers, waiting your turn to play, was often as much fun as the game itself. I felt I had to include some of the "Bleacher Chatter" in this book. They are merely diversions scattered throughout and have little to do with the story line, but are actual comments often overheard.

PART ONE

March 2017

CHAPTER ONE

Aim for a drop shot that has a considerable arc on it,
which peaks somewhere over the kitchen on your side of the net
and drops across the net.

Esther Conner, who is an expert at the drop shot, takes it to the limit when she drops along with the ball, as in DEAD, on the pickleball court at her Arizona retirement community. It really puts a damper on the Friday Night Round Robin.

Not to mention that it's also Friday Night Potluck. What a waste of the usual delicious favorites: Asiago wings, con queso dip, pork sliders, and double fudge brownies. It seems disrespectful to gorge after the incident. No one is more disappointed than Fred. He's ahead 10-8 but can't play the winning point, what with all the commotion on the court.

Esther's husband Mel is playing on another court when it happens and all play stops. He rushes to her side, but poor Esther has scored her last point (which technically would have been hers since the opponents didn't return that drop shot as she was going down).

Everyone assumes it's a heart attack. Yet, after the autopsy report, Detective Guy Lucchino starts hanging around the pickleball courts, as though observing the game, but mainly asking players how well they knew Esther. Rumor now is that her death was *not* an accident, but possibly intentional. Intentional because traces of poison were found in her system. Is this speculation or carry some truth?

Guy surmises from the comments of other pickleball players that Esther Connor wasn't the most popular person on the courts, but would someone kill her because she criticized their serve or backhand? Or because she shunned new players ranked 2.5 who innocently might have wanted to join a game with 3.5 players? Evidently, her brusqueness on the court offended someone.

Guy intends to find out who.

CHAPTER TWO

Everyone's gotta start from somewhere and even the best pickleball players in the world were beginners at one point.

"Listen to this," Angelina Popoff reads the sports page headline to June and Clara when they take a break from their Scrabble game. "'Pickleball is the fastest growing sport in America for seniors.' Last count was four million. Maybe we should get on the bandwagon."

"Who's on the wagon?" June asks. "For sure, it's not Harold. I saw him slamming down those martinis the other night at Wednesday Happy Hour."

"Not that wagon, June," Clara says. "Angelina means we should look into playing pickleball. Join the trend. Get in the 21st century. It might be good exercise and better than sitting on our duffs all day like we do playing Scrabble."

Angelina, June, and Clara play Scrabble twice a week. They used to play Mah Jongg on Mondays but decided to switch to Scrabble when their fourth player, Myra, died mysteriously — a mystery Angelina suspected wasn't a natural death as she began to put the clues together. The Mah Jongg Mavens saw it as an omen to perhaps move on to something else. They chose something that had never included Myra so her absence wouldn't be so noticeably missed.

Dear Myra, who always said the three of them reminded her of the Golden Girls. Spacy June was a Betty White knock off; Clara was brazen Dorothy. And Angelina? Well, she wasn't exactly Blanche, but in her mid-70s, she might pass for late-60s, especially if she lost a few pounds. With their varied personalities, when they got together it was often as entertaining as any sit-com. The Scrabble game takes place in Angelina's townhome kitchen, although they could play in one of the many activity centers their retirement community provides. As one resident says, these developments are "like summer camp on steroids for seniors."

"Now this is interesting," Angelina reads on. "'Pickleball was invented in 1965 as a children's backyard pastime on Bainbridge Island by Joel Pritchard, who in 1972 became the Lieutenant Governor of Washington. He and his buddies returned from a round of golf one afternoon and found their kids bored and restless, so they set out to create a game that would engage them through the lazy days of summer. They attempted to set up badminton, but no one could find the shuttlecock. They improvised with a Whiffle ball, lowered the badminton net, and fabricated paddles of plywood from a nearby shed. In the coming days both the kids and adults fell in love with the game and as they played the rules evolved.'"

Clara says, "Oh, great. One of those games where you make up the rules as you go along. We've all played with people who do that. They're usually losing and change the rules so they can win." She adds an *s* tile to *flower* to make it a plural with double score and says, "That's why I stopped playing Monopoly with Bobby Kokinda in fourth grade. Wonder what ever happened to him? Last I heard he blew up a gas station with a cigarette." She pops some peanut M & M's into her mouth from the array of snacks that accompany each game, including June's constant supply of Gummy bears to share.

June says, "What's a pickle got to do with anything?"

"That's interesting too" Angelina rustles the paper and reads on. "'Some sources claim that the name *pickleball* was derived from that of the Pritchard's dog, Pickles, but others claim it came from the term *pickle boat* referring to the last boat to return with its catch. Its crew of oarsmen is made up of leftovers of other boats. Just like the game was made with leftovers of other games. The dog came two years later and he was named after the game, not the game after him.'"

"Did I tell you that Frank and I won the mixed doubles in tennis back in the day?" Clara boasts. "Maybe he'll want to play too."

"I think you need four people," Angelina says.

They both look at June.

"Oh, no, not me. I wasn't very good in sports," June says. "But I still have my pep squad sweater. If you all decide to play I can cheer you on."

"Really? You still have your sweater?" Clara asks with a look of surprise. She peers at June as if she has spinach between her teeth. "That's weird."

June says, "Yes," with pride, totally ignoring Clara's inferred insult. "So it has a few moth holes, but every time I think I'm going to throw it out, I remember all the good times I had wearing it and just can't part with it." *Better than the memories of always being the last one chosen on the playground for any competition,* she recalls. Then she mumbles a Bible verse as she often does, "Many are called, few are chosen*, Matthew 20:16.*"

Angelina says, "Maybe Guy would like to join us. He's always saying he doesn't get enough exercise."

"Chasing bad guys doesn't burn up enough calories?" Clara asks.

Widower Guy, and widow Angelina became quite "friendly" as he worked on Myra's murder investigation. That *friendly* that was almost destroyed when Angelina decided to channel Agatha Christie to solve the crime herself, endangering herself and her friends.

Now she says, "Well, I didn't cheer or play sports but I think it would be fun to go to the open house they are having. Dedicating 12 new courts at the Fitness Center and giving free lessons."

"I love free," June says. "Don't they say 'never judge a gift horse by his teeth'?"

Clara is quick to correct her. "It's not judge, June. It's *look* and it's in the *mouth*. Not the teeth." In response to more of June's ongoing confusion of proverbs and idioms, Clara rolls her eyes as she reaches into the little velvet Scrabble pouch for a new tile.

Angelina just smiles inwardly. She enjoys the banter between Clara and June. To the casual observer it might appear that Clara and June do not get along. When in fact, Angelina knows they care for each other deeply, and also that June often purposely appears ditzy simply to get a rise out of Clara. At any rate, Angelina is thankful for their loyal friendship since she lost her husband, Peter, five years ago.

CHAPTER THREE

The best serve in pickleball is slow, deep and lob-like.

At the pickleball open house, the Fitness Center manager and the pro they recently hired demonstrate the game with a few members, making it look like a lot of fun. Angelina and Clara decide they want to give it a try. The next day they convince Guy and Frank, Clara's husband, to make up a foursome. To prepare, each of them watch YouTube videos for explanations and matches of the game.

June tags along, although she doesn't intend to play. Clara is relieved to see she isn't wearing her 50-year-old, moth-eaten pep-club sweater with the black and orange "Tigers" emblem. Actually, June looks quite put together, as usual, always ready for an excuse to get out of the house and afterward go to the clubhouse next to the courts. The Thursday night special is a pasta station with your choice of red or white sauce.

The foursome, armed with their new paddles and new, florescent yellow whiffle pickleballs, assume their positions on the court.

Angelina says, "I think he said the person in the northwest corner starts the serve. Because that's where the game began … in the Pacific Northwest."

They all look around in each direction as if there were a guiding star to point them northwest when Guy says, "Angelina is in the northwest corner."

"And don't forget to say the score each time before you start," Clara says.

From the sidelines, sitting close to the court, June says, "How can you say the score before you even start. There is no score."

"You say, 'zero, zero,' and then you tell which server you are," Clara says, somewhat annoyed that June is already interrupting their play.

Angelina, not wanting to break any rules before she even begins, says, "Zero, zero. I guess I'm server number one?"

"No, Angelina, the first service is always server number two. Remember what the pro said."

"That doesn't make sense to me."

Frank pipes in, "It's so the first team to serve doesn't have the advantage of having two servers before the other side even gets a chance to serve. Maybe that will help us remember."

Angelina serves the ball cross court to Clara. The ball goes over the net but lands short of the designated court. "Try again. We can have do-overs till we get it in the right court," Clara says. "That landed in the kitchen."

June laughs and yells, "The kitchen? There's a kitchen in pickleball? Is this a sport or a cooking show?"

Clara glares at June. "Junie, please don't be a commentator. It's very distracting."

June knows when she's been reprimanded. She mutters under her breath, "Sticks and stones will break my bones; names will never … well, yes, names hurt too. Or gather moss or something like that …." She pouts for a minute and then gets caught up in the fast-paced ball going back and forth across the net until Frank hits one very hard and it bounces off the back wall.

Guy shouts, "Out! Our point." Guy and Angelina switch positions on the court and Angelina serves again.

"Say the score, Angelina," says Clara. "Yours first, then ours, then server."

Angelina takes a deep breath and says, "One, zero, two." They all cheer at her successful score recitation.

The next play Angelina lands a good serve and Clara returns it with a hard slam. Guy stops the game. "Sorry, Clara, you forgot to let it bounce. First return has to bounce."

Clara hits her free palm against her forehead. "Duh, I forgot. Your serve."

When it's Frank turn to serve, he lands a perfect one the first time and they have a few volleys until Frank slams one low, right at Angelina's feet, which she can't return. He seems proud of himself as he says, "They say to aim for the shoelaces."

"Shoelaces? Everyone has Velcro these days," June mutters from the bleachers.

Frank starts to walk to the other side for another serve when Guy says, "Not so fast, Frank. I think you stepped in the kitchen on that volley shot. You can only step in if it bounces."

Now it's Frank's turn to say. "Oh man, crazy rule. You got me."

June knows she's not supposed to comment, but says to herself, *Serve can't go in the kitchen. Frank can't go in the kitchen. What good is a kitchen no one can go in. I guess there's always take-out.*

They continue to play until Frank and Clara win with a score of 11-6. They all come to the net and reach their paddles out to touch each other's, as they saw the teams do on YouTube.

"At least you didn't get pickled. You got out of the jar," Clara says.

"What's that supposed to mean?" June calls from the sidelines.

"Pickled means you didn't score one point," Clara says and then, "Rematch?"

They play two more games and all agree it's a good start and enough for the first time. "That was fun," Angelina says. "Wouldn't you say so?"

"I love it," Clara agrees. "What do you guys think?" She looks at Frank.

"I would do it again." he replies.

"I'm in," says Guy. "Maybe we burned enough calories to have seconds on pasta. You all go on in to the clubhouse. I'll be there shortly."

"Come on, June." Angelina says.

June gathers her purse and Gummy bears and says, "Yes, let's head to a real kitchen. One we're allowed to step in."

Guy stands on the top tier of the bleachers and looks over the courts. Several are in use. People laughing on one court. The distinct sound of staccato thwacks of a paddle hitting a hard plastic ball. The weather is typical of an Arizona day in March: 72 degrees, a cloudless blue sky and no humidity. Seems too idyllic for a murder but years in the business has taught him that even the most gruesome of crimes can take place in beautiful settings.

CHAPTER FOUR

After dinner, Guy drives Angelina back to her townhome not far from the clubhouse. When they pull into her driveway, she turns to him, "Would you like to come in for a nightcap?"

"I would never refuse any part of that invitation." He smiles as he turns off the ignition and covers her hand resting beside his.

"There are parts?" she asks, as she looks at his long, tan fingers, which for some reason have great appeal to her.

"Your company *and* the nightcap. But if I only get one, I would choose you." Guy became smitten with Angelina during the past year, and although her insatiable curiosity on every case he investigates drives him bonkers, he can't resist that part of her either. He finds himself thinking of her throughout the day and she's often his last thought before he falls asleep. He considers it a blessing to find someone he cares about again after losing Monica to breast cancer. It's a different kind of caring for Angelina than the love he had for his wife of 38 years but quite nice and often very surprising. The butterflies, the anticipation of seeing her and the deep longing for intimacy someday. So far, they are taking what she calls "baby steps."

The last time she used that term, he asked when they could advance to "teenagers" or at the very least "toddlers." She had just smiled as she rubbed the stubble she loved on his swarthy Italian cheek, as if that would pacify him. He hoped, that she too surely felt the rush of hormones so similar to those after dates in high school. She had said, "Our friendship is so nice. What if we move too fast and it doesn't work out? Then we've lost a beautiful friendship. One I don't want to give up at this point."

"Me either," he had said. "And some things are worth waiting for."

Although he retired from the force many years ago in his mid-seventies, he agreed to take on special cases, if needed, especially after Monica passed. Something to fill that void of empty hours consumed with grief. He knew he was starting to have feelings for Angelina when he was working the Myra Anderson case, but it wasn't until he thought Angelina was in danger herself that he realized what a loss it would be to not have her in his life. So he's willing to let her set the pace and simply enjoy the journey.

"Coffee, a beer or wine?" Angelina asks now as they walk into her townhome.

"A cup of decaf sounds good right now. Had enough wine with the pasta."

As Angelina fills the Keurig container, he pulls his favorite mug out of the cupboard and hands it to her, obviously at home in her kitchen. Angelina stands beside the Keurig as it fills and he suspects she'll soon be asking the questions he knows are coming. Questions he is not at liberty to answer.

When they are both seated at the table, Angelina confirms his thoughts. "So, this case of Esther Connor. Was she poisoned? That's the rumor, you know."

Guy says, "You know I can't discuss this with you. But if you want to share what you're hearing, I'm all ears."

"If I share, will you?"

"Probably not." He shakes his head with a sly smile.

She gives him a glance that indicates *not fair*. Then she says, "Sorry, I don't have any suspects yet for you, but what I'm hearing from some of the pickleball players, who also play

Canasta on Wednesdays, is that she was not the most popular lady on the court."

"And why is that?"

"They say she was condescending to beginners, hard to partner with — as in not forgiving when shots were missed or badly played, that sort of thing."

"That's the impression I'm getting also. Do you know if she had a close circle of friends?"

"They say … again those *they* people," Angelina rolls her eyes. "*They* say off-court she is— I mean … *was* as pleasant as can be. In fact, went beyond in helping others."

Guy takes a sip of coffee and then says, "Do *they* say anything about her family?"

"I don't know much about that. I don't think they have children, but I've heard that her husband, Mel, is one nice guy. Off and on the court. He might be nice, but isn't the husband always the first suspect?" she asks.

"You're reading too many mysteries, Angelina." Guy shakes his head, but inwardly smiles as he knows she will be relentless throughout his investigation and he actually likes bantering with her. Although Guy, like most widowers, had many invitations to dinner at the homes of attractive single women, starting a new relationship had no appeal to him until he met Angelina. Although in her 70s and a bit on the chubby side, he felt an immediate attraction to her warm and witty personality. Perhaps also because she didn't appear to have a marriage agenda like the younger women leaving casseroles at his doorstep.

Now he takes a last sip of coffee and goes to the sink to rinse out his cup. "Well, thank you for your information. That might be valuable down the road."

"So in return …?" Angelina asks.

"In return, I'm going to hit that road. Thank you for the coffee … and for including me in your new passion. Pickleball. I think it's going to be fun."

"Me too. And it's going to get us off the couch. Up and moving."

"Well, I wouldn't mind a little passion on the couch too," Guy says and winks.

She walks him to the door and they hug. Their hugs seem to last longer each time and as she pulls away gently, Guy tips her chin and kisses her softly. "One for the road. *Buona notte.*" *Good night.* He often injects phrases with his limited Italian vocabulary, summoning what was spoken in his childhood home.

She responds with *good night* in her native Bulgarian, as has become their custom. *"Leka nos."* Angelina closes the door and leans against it with a contented smile.

CHAPTER FIVE

Always choose the shot that keeps your opponents toward the back of the court.

Guy meets with the Fitness Center manager, Jeff, hoping he has a list of all the people who were on the pickleball court the Friday night Esther died. He asks, "Was there a sign-up sheet?"

Jeff says, "Yes and no. There is a hold-the-court system, but not everyone uses it yet. We're still working out the kinks. And some of our senior members are not what you might call computer-savvy." He rolls his eyes. "I can give you names of people who *did* hold a court that night. But some people show up for the Friday Night Potluck without signing up, hoping there will be a spot for them to play. The other thing is that at that late hour members can walk onto any empty court that's available, and I would have no way of knowing who that was. They're supposed to check in at the front desk but some don't."

"So you might have a partial list."

Jeff says, "Yes, I could compile a list of those players. I guess you could ask them who else they remember being there."

Guy nods his head. "It's a start."

Jeff goes on, "Keep in mind, however, that there are often people on the sidelines who are not playing, just walking by to watch the games or perhaps the spouse of one of the players. We would have no way of knowing who those might be."

By the time he leaves the Fitness Center, Guy has a list of names and contact information and begins his inquiries one at a time.

"Were you on the court the Friday night that Esther passed? Did you know Esther? Would you say you were friends or just an acquaintance? Did you ever see Esther off the pickleball court, as in other club activities? How would you describe her? Can you think of anyone she might have had a disagreement with recently? Do you, by chance, know who returned Esther's pickleball bag to her house?"

By the time he finishes interviewing 16 people, they confirm his original suspicion that Esther was not the most popular person on the court. He deduces that she was admired, or perhaps respected, for her mastery of the game, but not for her social graces or manners. Three of the ladies, Christine, Deborah and Nicole, who were in one of the private classes Esther taught had the kindest things to say about her. The comments they gave were so similar he wondered if they had met and both agreed on what to say.

"She would be the first person to help you in any way she could. Off the court, that is."

"A good coach if you could handle her criticism and somewhat gruff manner."

"She would give you the shirt off her back."

Of the three, Christine seemed quite nervous but he knew from countless interviews through the years that some people, although perfectly innocent, get flustered in talking to the police or a detective.

CHAPTER SIX

In spite of her alleged unpopularity, Esther's Celebration of Life is well attended.

Seated in the first row beside Esther's husband Mel are good friends Hank and Betty Harrison. Many others from the pickleball community are there, including those who attended the clinics Esther graciously taught at no charge. Seated together in the second row are Christine, Deborah and Nicole, all younger than Esther but old enough to qualify for a home in the retirement community. They were some of her first students and remained with Esther long after others had moved on. They became accustomed to her stern coaching manner and even regarded her somewhat as a mother figure who definitely wanted them to improve. It was almost as if Esther were two personalities … one on-court and one off. She was the first person, as many testified today, to take a meal to someone or drive a sick friend to radiation treatments.

At the end of the service, the three ladies in the second row, like the rest of the congregation, bow their heads for the Lord's Prayer. But two of them, unbeknownst to the other, is also saying a little private prayer of thanks. Thanks that the secrets only Esther knew about them were now also laid to rest.

CHAPTER SEVEN

Christine recalls the day it started. It was one of those unusually cold and windy days in Phoenix in January. They had all shown up at the pickleball courts, but one of them — she couldn't remember who — had said, "If you have to wear gloves, you shouldn't be playing pickleball. You should be skiing or better yet, sitting in front of a fireplace sipping a hot chocolate. With Baileys" They all agreed and decided to have breakfast at the new casino just 10 minutes from the courts.

After they had gorged on the breakfast buffet, they wandered around and put a few quarters in the slots. Christine planted herself in front of a poker machine, Deborah found the dollar slots, and Nicole wanted to spin the Wheel of Fortune. Esther wandered around and found a huge room already packed with senior citizens playing bingo. Christine recalled Esther's delight, "I love bingo! Let's check it out."

They could play bingo for three hours for as little as $25, so they all joined in. Although no one won anything, they had had a lot of laughs trying to keep up with the caller and the weird variation of games they played —101 ways to get bingo.

On the way out, Christine dropped three dollars in a dollar slot machine. Bells and whistles began piercing the air. She hit a jackpot. One thousand dollars! All four of them started laughing and screaming. She winced now to think of how much fun it had been. If only she had known what disaster it would lead to.

She found herself thinking of the casino at odd times during the rest of the week. She never told her husband Ben about her windfall, stashing it away as her "mad money." Although Ben was generous, a girl never knew when she might need a little extra cash.

One Thursday while Ben was out of town, he called to say he wouldn't get home as planned that night but would be on the same flight Friday night. She distinctly remembered the call and that little thrill of freedom she felt as soon as she hung up. She put the chicken she had set out to thaw back in the refrigerator. She knew in that instant where she would be having her dinner: Wild Horse Pass Casino — only 10 minutes from home.

She played the slots that night and the poker machines. She took $100 out of the ceramic ladybug cookie jar where she had stashed her earlier $1,000 winnings and came home with $225. She was surprised when she looked at her watch and discovered she had been there over four hours. Yes, whoever said time flies when you're having fun, was right.

She returned the $225 to the ceramic jar. She was starting to believe the legend that ladybugs bring good luck. She envisioned future winnings and thoughts perhaps she would surprise Ben one day with something really special for the two of them.

She didn't mention to Esther, Deborah or Nicole that she had returned to the casino alone. Maybe it was because they had teased her when she won, saying she'd be hanging out there each week. Little did they know that in fact she did return and the "each week" turned into three times a week, sometimes four when Ben was traveling. Each time she went, she took a little more cash from the jar than the time before. Some days she won, others she lost, but overall, she kept it pretty even, able to fund her "casino" fun money from the red and black ladybug.

Then she hit a losing streak. And try as she might, she couldn't seem to get ahead or even back to breakeven. She was shocked the day she reached into the ladybug and there were no dollars left. She even turned it upside down and shook it vigorously. How could that be? She knew the odds were that her luck would return so she borrowed from the household account. It was only one hundred dollars. Shoot, that was cheap entertainment. She knew women who blew that much in one trip to the mall.

Now she was into their savings account and hiding the monthly bank statements from Ben. Thank goodness she was able to screen the mail when he traveled. She knew it was just a matter of time until she had a winning streak — she'd put it back and then some.

Then Ben started talking about transferring some of their savings into some high-yield bonds and Christine knew she was in trouble. There was now $2,000 missing from that account. She also knew winning $2,000 on the slots was a long shot, but she had heard that the poker tables in the back room had some high stakes. Maybe she'd try it — just once. When she won, she'd return the savings and stop.

To prepare, she watched poker games on TV and YouTube. She felt confident she knew the game, the strategy, and how to play Texas Hold 'Em. She withdrew another grand and headed for Wild Horse Pass Casino. But as the cards were dealt to her that night, her palms were moist, and her stomach was full of butterflies.

Her first wagers were small,l and she won a few hands. Her confidence was gaining, and she began risking higher bets. She was dealt two kings. *A good sign.* She entered the pot and raised it with half her chips. All the others at the table folded except the young man across from her with the Yankees baseball cap and tattoo on his forearm. He looked too young to even be there. He couldn't be that experienced.

Then came the flop. A king, an ace and a ten. *Yes, her luck was changing. She could feel it.* She now had three kings. She made a good-sized bet and tattoo boy called her. *Maybe he had an ace? Hopefully not three aces.*

Fourth Street came and it was another ten. *Yes!* Now she had a full house so she made another rather large bet. He called her again. She wasn't worried about him having pocket aces, because she felt he would have raised her if he did.

The River card was laid. A dud. A six. She shoved her remaining chips to the center of the table and felt sure tattoo boy would fold now. But he didn't, he called her. With a smile on her face she turned over her cards to reveal her full house of kings full of tens. The boy smiled back at her and promptly turned over his pocket tens to reveal he had four-of-a-kind.

Her heart sank when she saw the four tens. She was stunned, having never put him on pocket tens . She mumbled, "Nice hand," got up and turned away so no one would see the tears stinging her eyes. The monotonous sound of the slots that were at one time so welcoming now sounded like a shrieking reminder that she had lost all.

As soon as she left the table, she felt the bile starting to rise in her throat. She ran to the ladies' room and slammed into the first stall she came to. She got there just in time to pitch the contents of her stomach. As she flushed the toilet, the realization that her plan to replace the money was also going down the drain. She left the stall and splashed cold water on her face. When she returned to the casino, she headed for the free coffee bar when she heard a familiar voice.

"Christine, what a surprise," Esther greeted her with what seemed like unusual delight.

"Oh, I just had some time to kill. Thought I'd get out of the heat." Then thinking no one comes to a casino alone but an addict, she added, "I was supposed to meet a friend here but she couldn't come at the last minute. How about you?"

"My Aunt Irma is visiting from Pasadena. I knew she'd just love the bingo — bless her heart. She can hardly hear the numbers. I feel like I'm the caller. I have to repeat each one. Driving the people around me crazy, but she's having a great time. Come and meet her."

Christine dutifully followed Esther into the bingo parlor, met Aunt Irma, and then drove home in a fog wondering how she was going to explain any of this to Ben. He would not be forgiving. Then in desperation, she thought, perhaps running into Esther was a sign — a sign that someone could help her.

The next day she called Esther inviting her for coffee when Aunt Irma left town. She assumed Esther had a generous savings account as she often spoke of different investments she was making. It was a long shot but one she felt she had to try.

As they settled in at the kitchen table, Christine said, "Esther, I'm in a jam. I have a terrible confession to make, and I didn't know who else to turn to. I hate to ask you, but Ben would never understand. You know his dad was an alcoholic and he abhors people who are addicted to anything."

Esther looked surprised. "Christine, I've seen you have a glass or two of wine but it's surely not addiction. Are you a closet drinker?"

"No, worse." Christine turned her head aside, ashamed to face Esther. "I'm addicted to gambling."

"Gambling? How? When?" Esther asked.

"It started with that $1,000 win. The day we all went together. It was so easy and so much fun, I just had to go back. And I kept winning. But then I started losing and I couldn't stop until I won it back. But I didn't stop, and I didn't win." The tears were streaming down her face now.

"It's become an obsession and now I'm in deep trouble with our savings account. I can't let Ben know and he's about to discover the missing funds. Any day now. But I've got it all figured it out. I'm going to get a job. It will keep me too busy to go to the casino and allow me to pay back my debt. My debt to you that is, if you'll loan me the money?" She gave Esther a pleading look.

"How much do you need?" Esther asked.

"I hate to ask you, but you know I'll pay you back. I swear Esther, I will. I don't have anyone else I can turn to."

"How much?" Esther asked again. Christine looked down into her coffee cup as a tear fell into it. She was so ashamed. She mumbled something as she reached for a napkin to wipe her eyes.

"Christine, darling, I can't hear you."

"Three thousand dollars." She covered her eyes with both hands and her shoulders shook with sobs.

There was a moment of silence that seemed to last forever and then Esther walked to the entry foyer table where she had set her purse. She brought it to the kitchen table and pulled out her checkbook and, to Christine's amazement, started writing.

Esther tore the check out of the checkbook and slid it halfway across the table but kept her fingers on it. "Christine, just promise me, you won't return to the casino?"

"I promise. Thank you so much. You just saved my marriage."

"And you'll call me if you get the urge?"

"Of course."

"Good." She slid the check to Christine. "Now, let's talk about what kind of job you'd like to get. And this *other matter* is just between us."

Later at Esther's Celebration of Life, Christine was ashamed of her own relief. That now she would not have to pay back the rest of the money she owned — $2,500. But had Esther told anyone of her debt?

Hopefully the secret Christine had confided in her was put to rest, as was Esther.

CHAPTER EIGHT

Deborah grew up the youngest of six children. Her father worked as a laborer at the steel mill and although they always had plenty to eat and a roof over their heads, Deborah wore hand-me-downs from her two sisters most of her school days. She was a pretty girl as a teen, but she didn't seem to know it. What she did know was that she lived in a neighborhood where cheerleaders or homecoming queens were scarce. She got in with the wrong crowd in high school and soon was doing whatever it took to belong. Things she knew were wrong.

The shoplifting started with a dare for simple things like a birthstone ring from the dime store, a fake amethyst for her mother. *Surely if you stole a gift for your mother, you wouldn't be punished, would you?* The fear of getting caught and then the relief of not getting caught became addictive. And she thrived on the admiration of her friends with each successful steal. It was a touch of excitement in her dull, boring existence as she bragged of her conquests, often giving the trinkets to her friends to further guarantee their friendship.

After high school, Deborah took a secretarial course and landed a job as a receptionist for a small law firm. Still living at home, she now had money to buy her own pretty clothes, even some jewelry. But every once in a while, she couldn't resist picking up a bauble that was more than what she could afford with her weekly paycheck. The thrill was even greater than when in high school because the stakes were higher. If caught, she would surely lose her good job and the financial freedom she was beginning to enjoy, not to mention suffer a possible stint behind bars.

Steve was a single attorney in the firm, fresh out of law school. He took her to dinner after they worked late one night on a brief. After that, he made a point to stop at her desk each day with a funny comment or special look.

They were married just one year later, and the first baby came 11 months after the day of their wedding. The second arrived a year later. Deborah knew her future was secure. Steve was smart and ambitious and there was no doubt he would make partner. She truly appreciated the beautiful lifestyle he was providing.

So, she never understood why, when she walked past a jewelry counter, she felt herself drawn to it. Longing to see if she could add just one more sparkle to her "special" bling-bling collection. One she could now afford to buy for herself but with not nearly the thrill of the escapade.

When the babies were one and two and she was out shopping alone for the first time in months, she couldn't resist the urge when it came upon her. It was just a baby's golden cross. *If you stole something religious, you couldn't be punished, could you?* She made it out of the store with the familiar adrenalin surging.

And then nothing — no urges for years, long after the children were gone. She was surely cured. Until that one Christmas. The store was crowded, and the clerks at the jewelry counter looked frantic. Everyone was trying on different items. Someone had left a tennis bracelet on the counter that should have been returned to the locked glass cabinet. Deborah touched it and laid it across her wrist. Lovely. So many people milling around. She wasn't the one who had asked to see it. No one would associate her with it. She held it around her wrist and clasped it shut. She held up her arm and looked at it in the mirror on the counter. No one was behind her, the salesclerk was busy on another counter, and the people on either side had their backs to her. And there was no bar code on the price tag. It was too easy. Too tempting. She let it slip down her left arm into her coat sleeve and waited a moment. No one seemed to notice her. Casually clasping the sleeve of her left arm at her wrist to secure the bracelet, she walked to the edge of the counter.

Her heart was beating quickly now. A rush of adrenaline. An announcement came through the Christmas music and startled her for a moment. "Shoppers, we will be closing in five minutes. If you wish to purchase something, please proceed to the nearest register." Several browsers rushed to the counter, almost knocking Deborah off balance, but still no one seemed to notice her. No one asked if she needed help or would she like to purchase the bracelet that was now sliding further down to her elbow as she raised her left arm. She let the shopping bag on her right arm slip to the right elbow so she could grasp her left arm close to her body. She could feel the bracelet against the crook of her elbow. She moved to the exit slowly, even stopping to browse. No one seemed aware of her. Soon she was out of the jewelry department and headed for the door to the parking lot. Her heart was beating quickly, and the familiar adrenaline was surging like the old days. She was only a foot from the door, and then, big as life, out of nowhere, she heard her name.

"Deborah, last minute shopping?" And there was Esther, all five feet, 10 inches of her hovering over Deborah, almost hugging her, so pleased to see her. In a split second, startled at the sound of her name, Deborah moved her left arm down and gasped as the bracelet fell out — with the delicate price tag in plain view. She was so near the door, there was no mistaking that she meant to leave with it. They both stared as it hit the floor, as if it were a bomb about to explode.

Then flustered and breathless, Deborah babbled, "Oh, that clerk was in such a hurry, she didn't even take off the price tag. I just splurged and bought myself a little Christmas present. I do that each year. I guess it's silly, isn't it, when I could just wait till the day after Christmas and probably get it half-price." She knew she was rambling, and she could feel her cheeks burning and her hands perspiring.

Esther just stared at her in the strangest way, as if she were trying to see something on her face that shouldn't have been there — like an ugly mole — and then she smiled with her mouth, but her eyes kept searching, deeper into Deborah's soul.

Then Esther said, "Oh, I don't think it's silly at all. It's so easy to get caught up in the buying frenzy, isn't it?" And then she continued to look, as if waiting for Deborah to say something.

"Esther, I'm so late. I should have been home an hour ago. See you Tuesday at pickleball?"

"No, remember, we're not playing until after Christmas."

Deborah ran out the door, bracelet in her hand, almost tripping over a stroller with a baby in it. Esther just stood there watching her go.

The incident was not referred to again. Deborah didn't wear the bracelet anywhere she thought she might see Esther. They never discussed it but somehow Deborah suspected that Esther knew it was stolen and often caught her looking at her in a strange way. While waiting for a pickleball court to open, sitting in the bleachers, Deborah would often feel Esther's eyes on her.

If Deborah returned her stare, Esther would politely look away as if she had been caught doing something wrong, but the last time, she didn't look away. She just kept looking at Deborah and said nothing. Deborah's palms became wet and her pickleball paddle almost slipped out of her hand.

Now focusing on the framed photograph of Esther on the Memorial Table, Deborah thought, "My terrible secret is finally safe."

CHAPTER NINE

When you're playing against a left-right combination, hit to the middle of the two players and hit slower balls, increasing odds of opponents confusing themselves.

Guy, Angelina, Clara, and Frank play another round of pickleball the following week. Their serves are improving, getting them in the correct quadrant more often than not, their scorekeeping is getting easier, although Frank normally forgets that the first server in the game is always server number two. And just as he announces the incorrect number, in the middle of his back swing, Clara reminds him that he is a two, which always throws him off and they lose the serve. The very reason some married couples don't play together.

Guy, in an effort to keep the peace, says, "I think the first server can also say *start.*"

June usually accompanies them, sitting on the sidelines, chatting with those waiting to rotate into a court. By the end of the match, it seems she knows something personal about each player. Where they grew up, how long they've been in Arizona, what they did before they retired. Her sweet demeanor is so non-threatening that people open up to her easily. Not to mention that she always has a bag of Gummy bears in her purse, which she offers willingly to share with her bleacher companions.

Having not played the game, the activity on the court is often confusing to June. She asks of the lady next to her, "So it seems there's a lot of shuffling around on the court. Front, back, left, right. How does one know where they're supposed to be or go?"

"Well, it's easier when you're playing, but it looks confusing if you're an observer. You really should try it. It's fun."

"I'm not very coordinated. And for sure I'm not competitive," June says with a sweet smile.

"Oh, you don't have to be competitive. Just play for fun."

"Well, I'm not so sure. Just yesterday, in my Bible study…we're in first Corinthians," she says, as if that explains everything. "It says, *Do you not know that in a race all the runners run, but only one gets the prize? Run in such a way as to get the prize."*

The lady next to her smiles politely but hastens to leave, as June discovers most people do when she starts quoting the Bible. June can't resist one more comment to the lady's departing back, "That's in chapter nine, verse 24." Then she mutters to herself, "You can lead a horse to water, but … but no use crying over milk … or a wayward horse."

BLEACHER CHATTER

"Did you hear about the accident on Shadow Lane yesterday? Lady driver had her dog in her lap .Got distracted Must have looked down and ran right through a garage. Luckily no one hurt. Not even the dog."

"I thought I heard the sirens. You know what they say when you hear them."

"What?"

"Another golf-cart for sale."

"Oh, that's terrible, sick humor."

"Sick, but sadly true in these retirement communities. 911 on speed dial."

"And estate sales every weekend. Boy, are they ever professional. The first one I went to, I couldn't believe how they were selling everything. I mean everything. There was an open kitchen junk drawer with a price sticker on the clean unused scratch pads."

CHAPTER TEN

Keep your eye on the ball. If you focus on making a noise when you hit the ball,
your shots will improve. Some players focus on the holes in the ball.

Guy makes it a point to go to the pickleball court frequently, on the pretense that he wants to watch the 4.0 players in order to improve his game. But Guy is watching a lot more than the game. He walks up and down the sidelines, making note of the many bags hanging on the fence, with different logos such as Nike, High Sierra, Athletico, Babolet. Some water bottles are left on the bleachers or on the ground while others are in the side pockets of the bags.

Many of the bags are of the exact same design, Nike being the most popular, although they often have distinguishing features such as a baggage tag or a special towel attached. Last year one player, Marita, a skilled sewer and quilt maker, made custom towels for players with their names embroidered on them.

But in Esther's case, Guy suspects, someone made a very custom design on her water bottle, or *in* her bottle, possibly exchanging the entire bottle for one that contained a poisonous substance.

Guy notices that there is certainly opportunity for this to happen as all the bottles are left out with easy access and while a person is playing, they don't seem to pay attention to what is happening on the sidelines. A person motivated to commit a crime could do so easily by becoming familiar with the intended victim's water bottle, especially if it was not a plastic generic see-through kind, from the local Safeway, Frys or Basha's grocery.

As soon as the forensic postmortem toxicology report found poison in Esther's system, Guy pays a visit to her home and asks Mel if he still has the water bottle she was using the day she fell on the court. Mel, still grief-stricken, can hardly answer the question. His shoulders are slumped and there are dark circles under his eyes as if he hasn't slept for days.

"I'm not sure. The day is a blur to me now. Someone calling 911, the ride in the ambulance. I didn't even take time to grab my own bag, let alone Esther's. Someone must have brought them both to the house later."

"Do you know who that might have been?"

"No." Mel shakes his head. My guess would be Hank. I know he was playing that night and his wife Betty always brings food to the Round Robin."

"I'll check with him. Are the bags here now?" Guy asks.

"Yes, in the garage."

"Have they been used since that day?"

"Mine has. As hard as it is to go to the courts, I've been playing pickleball just to get out of the house. The walls were closing in on me."

"Can you show me where Esther's bag is?"

Guy follows Mel to the garage, which is spotless and orderly. Large storage cupboards line one wall and wire storage bins hang from the ceiling with what must be Christmas décor in red and green crates. The floor has a spotless epoxy finish. His car is parked on one side and a golf cart on the other. One wall is a display of memorabilia. Plaques of golf tournament winnings, a poster of the Kansas City Royals 1985 World Series win, a variety of Kansas car license plates with tags from previous years.

"Nice wall," Guy comments. "My Dad saved all his old plates too — from Illinois."

"I was going to get rid of all this stuff when we moved here and downsized. But Esther insisted I keep everything from my *man-cave* as she called it. She knew it meant a lot to me." Mel shakes his head with a sorrowful expression.

Mel walks to the peg board and points to a red and black pickleball bag with a Nike logo. There is a water bottle in the side pocket that has a red knitted wrap around it with some sparkly little silver jewels on it.

Guy says, "Did you empty her water bottle before you hung up this bag?"

Mel shakes his head and looks confused. He says, "I haven't done anything. I don't even remember hanging it up. I couldn't bear to see her personal items so I haven't even unzipped it. I know she carried Chapstick, lipstick, and lotion. She always had a box of bandages and sunscreen. She was like a walking pharmacy … but not enough in there to save herself." He turns his head away and Guy sees him brush one eye.

Guy says, "I'll need to take the bag and water bottle in as evidence."

Mel looks surprised and for a minute Guy thinks he's going to refuse. *Is Mel protecting himself? Is he going to prove the theory that like so many cases, murder is at the hands of a family member?*

Then Mel says, "Of course, if it will help. Anything that will help."

Guy puts on gloves and pulls the bag down off the peg board as it seems Mel is reluctant to touch it.

Guy asks, "Other than you and your wife, do you know of anyone else who might have handled this bag?"

Mel looks confused. "I don't know who else would. Except whoever brought it back here. I went in the ambulance and then got a ride home from the hospital. I guess someone returned the golf cart we drove that night. Usually leave the keys in it."

"Thanks, Mel. Sorry to bother you with these details and reminders of that day. I'll return the bag soon. And I have to ask you to come down for fingerprinting, just to eliminate yours from any others. You understand."

Mel says, "Of course," but seems to appear very flustered at the suggestion. This puzzles Guy, as it would be normal for Mel's prints to be on anything of Esther's and not any sort of accusation. Then again, he has just lost his wife. Tragically. No behavior is normal for him now.

As Guy walks back through the house to leave, he passes a desk and notices what looks like several journals in the left corner. Small books that people often use as diaries.

He asks, "Did Esther by any chance keep any kind of journal or diary that you know of?" He glances at the desk as he says this.

Mel walks to the desk and looks at it as if he is thinking. "I did the household accounts, paid bills and all that stuff." He picks up the two little journals. "These are hers. I'm not even sure what she used them for." He opens one and thumbs through it and shakes his head. "Still not sure."

"Mind if I take them?"

"Go ahead. I can't imagine they would tell you anything."

"One never knows."

As Guy is about to go out the door, he turns to Mel and says, "I don't know if I ever fully expressed my sympathy to you for your loss. It's a difficult time. I lost my wife a few years ago and as hard as this is for you right now, the old adage that time heals does have some merit."

"And how much time does it take?" Mel asks with a touch of skepticism in his voice.

"Obviously, it's different for everyone. In my case, my wife was ill for some time, so perhaps I was more prepared for her death. You, on the other hand, had no warning. No chance to say good-bye and now having to deal with a possible murder? It's a lot all at one time."

Mel sighs deeply as if finally someone understands. He takes Guy's hand and shakes it. "Thank you. Thank you so much."

CHAPTER ELEVEN

Two Months Prior to Esther's Death

True to her word, Christine found a job, putting her bookkeeping skills to good use, and she started making payments to Esther each payday. She was quite proud of herself for following through on what she said she would do.

Between training for the new position and going back to work, she didn't have much time for pickleball except on the weekends.

During one of the weekend matches she did play, Christine and Esther were sitting together on the bleachers waiting to rotate in. There weren't any others within earshot of them but Esther still spoke in a hushed voice to indicate a confidential conversation.

"I'm very proud of you. Getting a job, keeping up your payments to me and …," she hesitated "… and hopefully staying away from the casino."

Christine said, "I feel good about it too. Hardly any time to go even if I wanted to. Which, of course, I don't."

Which of course was a lie. She wanted to go very much. So much in fact that she did sneak over some evenings when Ben was out of town. Her earnings from her job were not that much but Ben, in his old-fashioned man-takes-care-of-everything frame of mind, had said, "I can provide whatever we need. Do whatever you want with your paycheck. You just go have some fun with it." So, although she still didn't reveal where she went, she continued her trips to the casino with what she interpreted as his *blessing.*

She avoided the poker tables as the last experience left a bad taste in her mouth and went from slot machine to slot machine. Her new favorites were Cleopatra and Rainbow Riches, which seemed to pay out more often than the others.

She soon discovered she could spend hours at a twenty-five-cent poker machine with a mere $20, often playing off her winning quarters. Four-of-a-kind gave her 125 more quarters. She made a vow to herself to limit any losses to $40 per casino visit and she would not get into trouble. It seemed very justifiable and as if she were in control. She even kept track of her winnings and her expenditures in a little notebook dedicated to that purpose with accurate accounting.

Then shortly after she had the little pep talk with Esther on the sidelines, the four ladies played a match and stood around chatting afterward, talking about when they might play together again.

"Anyone up for an evening match? Esther asked. "I like playing under the lights."

"I've read that exercise before bedtime is good. Makes for a good night's sleep," Deborah said.

Nicole said, "I'm good for that."

They all glanced at Christine for her response, and she said, "Sure, why not?"

Her hesitation caused Deborah to ask her jokingly, "Oh, you got better things to do when Ben's out of town?"

Nicole piped in, "Christine, I forgot to tell you I saw you at the casino last Tuesday. But we were just going into the seafood buffet and didn't want to lose our place in line. All the lobster you can eat. It's a great deal."

Christine could feel her cheeks burning and was afraid to look at Esther. *Caught, caught, caught in her lie.* When she did look up,

Esther was glaring at her with that stern look she gave someone when they missed what should have been an easy shot.

They all agreed to play again on Wednesday night and Christine left abruptly without looking at Esther again. As she was pulling out of the parking lot, Esther walked toward her car. She had no choice but to stop as Esther approached her window, or else she would run over her toes. Christine lowered the window and waited for the barrage that was sure to follow.

Esther just shook her head and said, "Christine, I'm so disappointed in you. Breaking your promise and worse yet, lying about it. Didn't you say you would call me if you got the urge?"

"I did. Yes, I did those things. I got the urge, I didn't call, and then I was ashamed to admit it. I'm sorry Esther. I don't know why. But I'm only playing with my earnings, not the household account. And I'm making my payments to you, so what's the harm?"

"The harm is that it appears to be addiction. And addictions usually spin out of control at some point."

"It's harmless, Esther. Just a way to unwind for a few hours. I know ladies who spend more money on their weekly trips to the mall, buying things they don't even need."

"And that's why they're called 'shopoholics,' another addiction," Esther replies. "I wanted to help you Christine, but now I'm not so sure I did the right thing. Perhaps I'm what they call an enabler."

"You'll get your money back. I promise."

"It's not the money I'm concerned about. If it was, I wouldn't have lent it. It's you."

"Well, please don't worry on my account. I'm fine."

"Maybe you need more support at home. Perhaps Ben should know where you spend your evenings."

"You wouldn't," Christine said. And she shifted into reverse so she would not run over Esther's toes when she left the parking lot.

She could feel her anger building as she drove home. Anger at

Esther for being so bossy, anger at herself for getting caught. Anger at the whole situation. Absorbed in her thoughts, she almost missed the slow down speed sign in the school zone. *Great, all I need now is a speeding ticket. That would cost a lot more than a night at the casino.*

But by the time she pulled into her own driveway, she knew she had to make amends with Esther so she wouldn't make good on her threat to let Ben know. Somehow, she had to stop Esther before she tried "to help" her.

CHAPTER TWELVE

Two Months Prior to Esther's Death

After a round of evening pickleball under the lights, Esther, Deborah, Nicole, and Christine went into the Country Club for the nightly special. There was a live band, and several couples were on the small wooden dance floor near the bar. They displayed a variety of dance styles, some of them looking like they were graduates of a Fred Astaire ballroom class while others were reminiscent of 8th graders who stood close together and barely shuffled their feet. The club often played the "oldies but goodies," and if it was an Elvis jitterbug from the 50s, often a group of women would dance together, hopefully enticing one of the men on the sidelines to ask them for the next slow dance.

As they observed one particularly awkward couple dancing, Esther said, "You know what's worse than a man who can't dance?" The other three didn't bother to reply, assuming this was a hypothetical question and Esther would give them the answer, which she did. "One who *thinks* he can dance."

At that moment the gentleman who inspired that remark passed in front of them, awkwardly gyrating, and they all smiled in agreement.

Deborah turned to Nicole, "Don't look now, but I think the guy in the tan sport coat at the bar is going to ask you to dance. He's been looking at you since we came in." Of course, all three of them turned immediately and looked. He smiled and waved at them.

Nicole blushed. “Oh my gosh, he’s old enough to be my father.”

“He’s nice looking though. And perhaps a sugar daddy wouldn’t be so bad, would it?” Christine said.

“How do you know he’d have sugar?” Esther asked.

Christine said, “First clue. Look at how he’s standing. He’s got that cocky, confident pose rich men do. And look at his loafers. He didn’t get those at Payless.”

Nicole laughed. “I think you’re right.” And when he raised his drink to his mouth, she added. “Even across the room, that watch looks like a Rolex.”

Christine says, “I, myself, prefer men who wear an Omega. You know, like James Bond. And I heard Buzz Aldrin did too. Astronauts are so sexy.”

Esther said. “You can tell a lot about a person by the jewelry they wear.”

She looked at Deborah when she made this remark. And it wasn’t the first time she made Deborah uncomfortable. It seemed every time they got together the first thing Esther did was look at Deborah’s wrist to check if she was wearing her tennis bracelet. Deborah found it quite annoying and was getting tired of it.

Christine said to Nicole. “So, what do you think? Going to dance with him when he walks over here?”

Nicole, recently divorced, said, “Sure, I’ll dance but that’s about it. I’m not ready for a relationship. Especially to someone that age. As my 82-year-old Aunt Gertrude says, “I don’t want to be anyone’s nurse or purse.”

They all laughed but Deborah was still squirming inside over Esther’s constant scrutiny and judgmental glances.

CHAPTER THIRTEEN

One Month Prior to Esther's Death

During one of the pickleball matches, Deborah, Christine, and Esther were sitting in the bleachers waiting for a court and waiting for Nicole, their fourth player, to arrive. Deborah said, "She's been kind of spacey since she's dating that new guy. What's his name? Darrell?"

"I think she really likes him, more than anyone she's dated since her divorce," Christine added.

"It's still too soon. You know those rebound things don't usually work out," Esther commented in her assured *I-am-usually-right* style.

Nicole rushed up to them, looking a little flustered but cheerful. "Sorry guys, hope I'm not too late. Oh, good, our court isn't open yet," she said with a sigh of relief. Then she waved her left hand in front of them, sporting a large ruby ring. "I couldn't wait to get here and show you this. I'm so happy. Darrell gave me this last night. He calls it a commitment ring." Her smile was huge.

"Wow," Christine exclaimed. That's quite the rock. Uh, I mean congratulations."

After Nicole told them how he dropped the ring into her martini glass and she was glad she hadn't swallowed it, they settled down and had a short discussion about whether or not they should wear jewelry while playing pickleball. Deborah didn't chime in at all, but kept glancing at Esther when she wasn't looking her way.

Nicole said to Deborah, "Why don't you ever wear that pretty tennis bracelet you got for Christmas? Saving for a special occasion?"

Before she could answer, Christine said, “Court’s open. Let’s go. See if that new bling- bling brings you luck on the court.” She tapped Nicole on her bottom with her paddle and then gave her a hug.

Deborah’s game was off. She kept thinking of the tennis bracelet, and after the match, she wanted to leave as quickly as possible, but Esther said, “Deborah, do you have a minute?”

“Sure,” she answered because she couldn’t think of any excuse fast enough.

Esther and Deborah walked to the parking lot together and stopped at Deborah’s car. From the stern look on Esther’s face, Deborah felt like she’d been stopped for a traffic violation. *Step out of the car, Ma’am.* As she feared, Esther talked about the day they ran into each other prior to Christmas.

“You know, Deborah I’ve never said anything. Wanted to give you the benefit of the doubt, but I’ve been thinking lately that it’s not right to overlook what I think was blatantly theft on your part. I know I might be risking our friendship with this accusation, but somehow …,” she paused, “… especially now with your face turning a deep shade of red, I don’t think I’m mistaken. Am I?”

“What are you talking about?” Deborah asked although she knew perfectly well what she was talking about. She was stalling for time to come up with a plausible reply.

“I’m talking about a visible price tag on that tennis bracelet when you were leaving Macy’s last Christmas. I can’t believe the sensors didn’t go off and alarm the whole store. I’ve thought about it several times and thought, well, it’s none of my business, but lately I think it *is* my business. You know people get away with little crimes, they are overlooked and next thing you know, it’s a bigger crime and someone says, ‘Gee, I had no idea he was a serial killer …’ although he killed all the cats in the neighborhood, which everyone failed to mention.”

“My gosh, Esther, I am far from a serial killer. Isn’t that a bit far-fetched?”

“So how long has this been going on? I’m sure that was not your first offense.”

“It’s not like it’s a Mom-and-Pop operation that would lose money. Those big chains, the mark up on jewelry is ridiculous.”

“So that makes it right?”

Deborah covered her face with both hands and when she lowered them, she was crying. "No, it wasn't right, and I haven't done anything since or years before. I stole cheap stuff from the dime store when I was a teen. I wanted to belong to this group of skaggy girls and they dared me. I don't know what came over me that day you saw me. I can certainly afford to buy the bracelet."

"I guess if you couldn't afford it, it would make some sense. But it doesn't. And your husband, a partner in a reputable law firm? What were you thinking?"

"I wasn't obviously."

"Have you considered counseling?"

"No, I told you. It hasn't happened in years." Deborah crossed her arms tight across her chest. "So what are you going to do? Turn me in? Have me return the bracelet? What do I need to do to make it right with you?"

'It's not me you need to make it right with. It's yourself. Or maybe you should do some community service. You could talk to teens about the dangers of succumbing to peer pressure that's wrong."

"I don't want to talk about this to anybody. I want to forget it ever happened. Can't you?"

"I'm not so sure I can."

With that, Deborah got in her car and slammed the door, leaving Esther standing there, knowing her time with Esther on the pickleball court was probably over. As was her friendship.

Driving home, Deborah realized pickleball was the least of her problems. What if Esther talked to her husband? *I wouldn't put it past her. This woman needs to be gone. The world would surely not miss one more busy-body do-gooder.*

CHAPTER FOURTEEN

Mel refuses the many invitations to dinner from friends. He finds it easier to stay home and watch TV, often in a state of numbness, rather than try to politely keep up a conversation that seems frivolous and meaningless now. Most friends stop asking after the first few refusals, but Betty, who became a good friend to Esther, is more persistent and he finally relents. Hank is also an easy guy to be around and he's thinking a home-cooked meal might be nice after so many Lean Cuisines and Healthy Choice dinners. Or liquid stupor.

Although it's an hour before he has to leave the house for dinner, he pours himself a drink to settle his nerves. Perhaps they would offer him one but what if they don't? Better to be prepared and if they do, two would do no harm. It could help him get through the evening and by the time he gets home, it will be bedtime. He would have made it through another day. And hopefully another night with no haunting dreams.

The enticing aroma of roast beef hits him as soon as Hank opens the door, and Mel feels the stirring of hunger pangs he has not experienced for days. It has also been a long time since he walked into a home that had signs of life. There's soft music in the background, some candles and a sense of homey comfort.

"Mel!" Hank says with exuberance, almost as if he's surprised to see him, "Come in, come in. So glad you can join us."

Before Mel can express his thanks, to his relief, Hank takes him by the elbow and leads him to a sidebar with several bottles of liquor. "What's your pleasure?" he asks. "Or if you'd rather, we have beer and wine."

Mel points to the bottle of Jack Daniels and says, "A Jack would be nice. Just a couple of ice cubes," he adds.

Betty comes out of the kitchen, wiping her hands on her apron. Mel feels a pang of sorrow at this domestic touch that reminds him so much of Esther. "Something smells wonderful," he says to Betty.

"I figured if you're like most guys, you like your beef. And potatoes and gravy too. There's nothing like comfort food when one needs comforting." Mel finds it interesting that some people avoid the subject of grief altogether while others, like Betty now, come right out and meet it head on. She says, "Enjoy your drinks. Dinner will be ready shortly," and she returns to the kitchen.

Hank motions for Mel to sit in one of the two easy chairs near the fireplace. He never understood why, when they were looking for homes in Arizona, so many had fireplaces but he came to appreciate how it took the chill off a cool evening, not to mention the ambiance it added to a room. And reminiscent of his Kansas home.

The two couples became friends when they discovered that in addition to their common interest of pickleball, they were both from Kansas. Although Betty didn't play as often, she and Esther did a lot of other things together. Crafts, lunches, an occasional movie. Hank was retired from many years at the Cessna manufacturing facility and Mel retired from the Collins School Bus manufacturers, but he rarely spoke of it and tried to divert the subject when it came up.

Betty comes into the room. "Who's hungry?" she asks.

Dinner conversation is pleasant enough, centering on the activities offered at the clubhouse. Betty prattles on about them, "I love playing Mexican Train dominos. And I'm trying to get Hank to go to the social dance class." She looks at Hank who is shaking his head *No* to Mel.

Mel says, "This is delicious, Betty," he says. "It's been some time since I've had a home-cooked meal."

"I figured as much," she says sympathetically. "Probably just one of the many things you miss about your Esther."

Mel looks down at his plate, nods with a wry smile as if to indicate yes, and when he looks up his eyes meet Betty's. Something causes him a moment of discomfort. Her expression looks totally inappropriate for the conversation. Is it his imagination or is her smile actually a smirk? As if Mel's sorrow is a good thing?

Then a genuine smile as she says, "And I'm sending some leftovers home with you. And next week Tuesday is taco night here. You must come back. I'll invite some of the others from the club over too. How would that be?"

They say their good-byes and Mel promises he'll return, although he thinks he'll try to find a way to wiggle out of it. He'd rather be home alone, nursing his grief, than making small talk.

Later that night just before he falls asleep, he recalls that strange look on Betty's face. It reminds him of the look one of the bully kids in his neighborhood had when his own pup, Maxi, was run over. As if he were glad that it happened. Mel never forgot that look and tonight he thought he saw it again. *But that doesn't make any sense. Perhaps I had too much Jack.*

Mel has a restless night of sleep. As he tosses and turns, in his waking moments he wonders, as he often did. *What were the odds that the one couple they were closest to were from Kansas? And not that far from Hutchinson. What if they knew of the accident? His involvement?* Now he not only has to deal with grief and the uncertainty of Esther's death but of his own past catching up with him. As nice as they were and as delicious as Betty's dinner was, he knew there was no way he was showing up for Taco Tuesday.

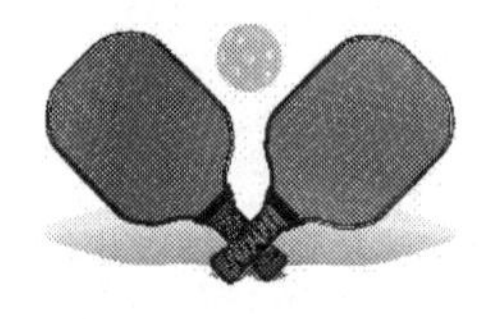

Married for so many years, Betty and Hank have established a routine after entertaining. Hank clears the table as Betty puts away leftover food. Hank pours himself a nightcap of bourbon and sips it as he leans against the counter while Betty begins to load the dishwasher.

"I think that went well, don't you?" Hank asks.

"Yes, his grief is quite profound As it should be. As it should," Betty says.

CHAPTER FIFTEEN

Although it's been more than a year since Angelina and Guy met, she still feels giddy and gets a thrill when he calls, when she hears his voice, especially the early morning calls as he has started doing.

His voice is still sort of raspy, like he's just woken up and it feels intimate even though they didn't spend the night together. In fact, they have never. Sometimes it's a text instead of a call. Always the same, "Good Morning Sweetheart." She keeps her phone under her pillow so she doesn't even have to get out of bed when she hears the early morning *ping*.

And often he's the last voice she hears before she falls asleep as they have been saying goodnight to each other also. *Buona notte. Leka nos.*

She's not sure where this romance (if you can call it that and she thinks she can), is headed but the nice thing is that it doesn't have to have a destination. It's quite nice just the way it is. *Baby steps.*

When she's being totally honest with herself, she knows she would like it to be more, but she's afraid. Afraid that if they take the next step and it's not right … well, then does one go back to being just friends? That's awkward. What if a bedroom scene goes terribly wrong? And there's the aging body thing. No one has seen her naked body since her husband passed. Old cellulite and skin wrinkled as crepe paper cannot be attractive, especially to someone who never knew the young body. Would she wear her big furry robe to bed and keep it bedside so she could slip in and out of it somehow before she ever got out of bed? Like Houdini? The thought of someone seeing her naked bouncy butt walk away was too appalling. And how about those frequent trips to the bathroom in the middle of the night? It was *all* just too much to think about.

For now, it's comforting enough to think someone cares about you. And if you are home safe. And at her age, if you made it through the night. Before Guy's calls, she often wondered how would anyone would know if she passed in the night? Her daughter calls and texts often but not at the same time each day.

Clara once told her, "Angelina, I'm going to call you each morning. I mean you could be lying on the floor disabled for hours before anyone missed you."

"Clara, that's very considerate but really not necessary. I'm perfectly healthy, and your calling each day to check on me, if you must know, makes me feel old and decrepit." Clara relented, although to Angelina it seems she does call more than necessary with lame excuses for the calls. It's obvious she is "checking."

Angelina wonders, "Should I tell her Guy and I talk morning and night? I don't think I'm ready for her to know that. Then she'll tell June and they'll act weird around him when he's with us and June will say something like, "Make hay while the sun shines." Except she'll get it all wrong and say something more like, "Make hay while opportunity knocks." Or "Opportunity gathers no moss."

Angelina smiles at the thought of June trying to play matchmaker because she knows she has her best interests at heart. Yes, heart. It's all about the heart. And now, after losing her husband Peter and never dreaming of finding love again at her age, Angelina's heart is full.

CHAPTER SIXTEEN

After warming up some leftovers Angelina has sent home with him from their last dinner together, which is almost every evening, Guy pours himself a small shot of his favorite night cap, Johnny Walker Red. He has his Food Channel shows recorded to watch after dinner, but first he pulls out the two journals he found on Esther's desk.

Although there are no printed dates on any of the pages, there are handwritten dates in the upper left-hand corner going back over a year. It looks like a "to-do" list with errands, calls, etc. There's a bullet dot beside each single space entry with an *x* through most of the bullets. Some don't have an *x* but an arrow, and he notices that those with an arrow are carried over to the next page.

He turns page after page seeing nothing noteworthy. He opens the second journal and in addition to more bulleted entries he sees notes on right-hand pages. At the top of one page there is an entry that says, "Christine $3000." Below that are dates and dollar amounts subtracted from the $3,000. Five entries of minus $100. He pulls out his own notebook and scrolls through it. *Same Christine I interviewed already? The one who played pickleball with Esther?*

He closes her journal, takes a sip of Johnny Walker and heads for his recliner and the remote. He has watched all his beloved Kevin Bacon DVD's so now he clicks on his current favorite food show, "Chopped."

CHAPTER SEVENTEEN

Angelina is, for the first time, including Guy in her Sunday night family dinner with her children. Her single daughter April, son Peter Jr., his wife Erica, and two grandchildren, Sam and Leslie.

Angelina is a bit nervous. Although she's told both children about Guy, they have not yet met him. Will they like him? Will he like them? Is it too soon? Not too soon after Peter's death? That's been five years, but is it too soon in her relationship with Guy? Will Guy see it as a sign of her wanting more than he might be ready for himself?

April has already given her blessing to Angelina dating again. Dating discussions were off limits for some time between the two after their quarrel over April's long-term relationship with Gary, where Angelina so rudely interfered and later regretted every minute of it. April finally forgave her mother's intrusion when she admitted to herself that her relationship with Gary was going nowhere.

"That's wonderful, Mom," she said when Angelina first told her about meeting Guy last year during Myra's murder investigation. Angelina didn't elaborate on how Guy saved her life because then she would have to admit she was prying into police business that was not her business.

And her son Peter Jr., like most guys, had little to say other than, "Great Mom. Nice to have someone to see a movie or have lunch with." Would they both be shocked that Angelina wanted more than a movie and lunch? Not only did kids no longer want your good china when you passed but they surely didn't want to hear details of your renewed sexual awakening while alive.

April arrives first and Guy follows shortly after with flowers and a bottle of wine.

"Trying to impress my daughter?" Angelina asks with a smile as she greets him with a small peck on the cheek.

"Guilty," he says. He hands the flowers to Angelina, sets the wine down on the kitchen counter, and walks toward April. "I'm so happy to finally meet you. Feel like I know you already from all the good things your mother has told me."

"Oh no, you can't believe any of that. She's quite biased."

"I get that. I have a daughter too, about your age. I think your mother and I try to 'one up' each other with our daughter stories." He glances at Angelina as if to see that this meets with her approval.

April says, "Is she here in Phoenix? You should have brought her." She glares at her mother. "Why didn't you invite her? After all it is Sunday family dinner."

Guy says, "She's in Chicago. Law school."

"A detective and a lawyer in the same family. Whoa. That has to make for some interesting conversations."

Guy laughs and is about to say something when the door bursts open and eight-year-old Sam bounds in and rushes to Guy. "Do you have a gun?" he asks, eyes wide with potential excitement.

"Sam!" his father says. Peter Jr. looks at Guy. "Sorry about that. I guess I shouldn't have told him you're a detective."

Guy laughs. "No problem. I'm used to that question. More from criminals than kids though."

Angelina smiles her approval as she sees Peter Jr. relax and then reach out to shake Guy's hand. "I'm Peter Jr. Call me PJ. Or should I just say, Sam's Dad."

"Where are the girls?" April asks.

"They had a baby shower to go to and one of Leslie's little friends was also going to be there with her mother. Sorry Mom, did I not tell you they weren't coming?"

Angelina hugs her son. "I don't think so, but it's not a big deal. I'll send some lasagna home with you for them."

"Lasagna?" Guy says. "My favorite."

Angelina says, "I think I'm brave to cook lasagna for an Italian whose mother probably made the best ever." She rolls her eyes. "I have a few things to finish in the kitchen. Why don't you pour yourselves some wine or whatever you'd like to drink and get acquainted?" She slips back into the kitchen but within hearing distance of their conversation. She doesn't want to miss a word of it.

During dinner they ask Guy where he grew up and encourage him to talk about his Chicago family. It's obvious he enjoys talking about the fire station his Dad worked at for many years. He in turn asks them about their jobs and interests. All while Sam keeps interrupting with questions about fire trucks and gangsters.

Sam asks, "Who's the scariest guy you ever met?"

'Oh, that's easy," Guy says. "I'd have to say my wife's father, the first time I asked his daughter out."

The adults laugh but Sam says, "I mean real bad guys, like crooks."

When it's time to leave, Guy doesn't linger, sensing that perhaps this is the one time of the week Angelina has alone with her children.

"Mom, he's charming," April says the minute Guy, Peter, and Sam leave.

Angelina blushes, "You think so?"

"Yes, and it's obvious you think so too. So how serious is this? Why have you waited so long for us to meet him?"

"Uh," Angelina shrugs her shoulders. "I'm not sure. I really enjoy being with him and it's so comfortable … but I'm a little bit afraid that if we move too fast it might all fall apart."

"Mom, that's silly." April says. Then, "Well, what do I know? My track record is not so good with men. But I'd say, hang on to that one. Seems like a really decent guy. Nice-looking too."

"He is rather handsome. He reminds me a little of Columbo who I've had a crush on ever since his TV series. Kinda swarthy, hair falling over his eyes, which I haven't figured out yet if they're blue or grey. Change all the time."

"I'm sure you're a good sounding board about his cases, as much as you love your mysteries."

"You would think so, but he's pretty closed about that. Right now he's working on the death of a lady on the pickleball court. Someone may have poisoned her."

"Really? Wow, that's one poor loser, wouldn't you say?"

"That's for sure." Angelina responds.

When April leaves, Angelina settles in her reading chair with Henry, her Garfield-like cat sprawled spread eagle on the back of the chair, legs dangling over each side. She picks up the book she recently purchased, *A is for Arsenic: The Poisons of Agatha Christie* by Kathryn Harkup. In spite of Guy's warning to not get involved Angelina thinks she should be doing a little investigating of her own.

CHAPTER EIGHTEEN

The dink shot is a slower, softer shot hit from the no-volley line that drops downward once it crosses the net and lands in the opponent's no volley zone.

Guy scans the pickleball membership list the manager of the Fitness Center gave him for anyone named Christine. He finds one with a check mark beside it indicating he has already spoken to her. The notes beside her name are that she, along with two others, Nicole and Deborah were in Esther's class and then they continued to play often as a foursome. Other than that, there was nothing noteworthy other than she said Esther was an excellent coach and off-court always willing to help someone.

Then he checks the list of players who signed in the night of Friday Potluck. Christine was there. Guy dials her number and when she answers, he asks if it would be possible to come by. He has a few more questions about Esther.

He hears hesitancy in her response, but she says, "Of course, Detective, but I can't imagine what else I can tell you."

"Would you like me to come to your home or would a coffee shop be better? It won't take long, I'm sure."

They agree to meet at a little diner that serves breakfast and lunch only, not far from the Fitness Center. Although the place is not busy mid-morning, Guy waits in a booth near the back for privacy. He orders a coffee and places Esther's journal off to the side.

When Christine arrives, he asks if she'd like coffee and signals the waitress to return.

"Thank you for meeting me. I'm just following up on a few things. Did I ask you before how long you have known Esther?"

"To be honest, Detective, I don't remember what we talked about. But I can tell you I've known her since she moved here. I guess a little over a year." She starts fidgeting with the sugar packet creasing the edges over and over.

"Did you meet through pickleball or did you know her before that?"

"We met at the court when she posted a flyer saying she would teach beginners. Nicole and Deborah and I all signed up."

"Did you spend time with her outside of pickleball?"

"Occasionally, we did some things together — maybe a bite to eat after a lesson or match." Christine fidgets with the sugar packet smoothing the edges between her fingers. "If you don't mind my asking, why are you asking me these questions?"

"I'll get to the point, Christine." Guy reaches for the journal and opens it to the page where he has placed a sticky tab. "This is Esther's journal and there's a page here with your name at the top. Well, I think it might be your name. Her husband couldn't recall any other Christine she knew. He and I might be mistaken, but you understand we have to check out every little thing. By chance, does the number 3,000 have any relevance to you with Esther?"

Christine feels her cheeks starting to burn and when she places her mug back on the table, her hand is shaking causing a few drops of coffee to spill over. She looks down at the spill and takes her napkin to wipe it. She doesn't answer immediately. When she looks up, Guy suspects there are tears in her eyes.

"Yes, Detective. I guess there's no point in lying about it."

"About what?"

"Esther loaned me $3,000. I was paying her back on a monthly basis."

"I see," Guy says. "It appears from the notations here that you made five payments of $100."

"That sounds right." She lets out a big sigh.

"Didn't you think that might have been important to mention when we first spoke?"

"I guess I should have said something. To be honest, I am quite embarrassed about the whole incident. The loan, I mean. It's not something I'm proud of."

"I see. Is her husband aware of this loan?"

"That I couldn't say. He has never mentioned it to me."

"Were you planning to tell him about it?"

She leans back in the booth and doesn't answer his question immediately, as if she has to consider what she is going to do. Then she says, "Probably not. After all, the money was from her, not her husband."

"So you were hoping, in essence that with her passing your debt was wiped out?"

"The thought had occurred to me."

"Were you having any difficulty making the payments?"

"No, you can probably see in that little book ...," she glances at it as if it's contaminated. "I made them quite regularly each month. The same day twice a month when I got paid. From a job I got mainly to pay her back. No other reason."

"It may have no bearing on this case, but can you tell me why you borrowed the money in the first place?"

Christine looks down and massages her forehead with her fingertips. When she looks up, she says, "I don't see what that has anything to do with ... with anything." Guy doesn't say anything, but waits. She lets out a deep breath and blurts, "I had a gambling debt I had to pay back. Esther was kind enough to help me, so ...." She stops talking here.

"So what, Christine?"

She starts twisting her wedding ring. "So my husband wouldn't know I took money from our savings account."

"Does he know now what has transpired?"

"Of course not. There's no need for that." She takes her purse and rises to leave. "Are we done here Detective? I've answered all your questions. And if you think I would harm Esther to wipe out a debt, you are sorely mistaken." She turns her back and walks away.

After she leaves, Guy makes a note in his tattered book, "The lady doth protest too much."

Sitting behind the steering wheel, Christine's fingers tremble as she inserts the key into the starter. *I should have known Esther would leave a paper trail somewhere, meticulous as she was. Now what?*

CHAPTER NINETEEN

"I know we can't talk specifics to your case," Angelina says to Guy.

"And what would the general subject be?" Guy asks, although he is well aware of what Angelina is referring to.

"Murder in general, poisons if we could be specific."

"Of course," Guy says, dabbing his mouth with the napkin after the last bite of sweet and sour chicken. They enjoy eating at one of their favorite restaurants, not only for the delicious cuisine but because it was where they had a first date. *Chino-Bandido*. The menu offers both Chinese and Mexican or a blend of both. As Guy always says, "One can hardly go wrong."

He never misses a chance to eat at a restaurant that's been featured on the Food Channel's "Diners, Drive-Ins and Dives." Last summer he drove as far as Flagstaff to go to Salsa Brava on historic Route 66 and declared it was worth it to try the chicken-stuffed sopapilla and their foot-long salsa station. And then he had to check out Diablo Burger. Not because it was on TV, but *USA Today* claimed it was one of the top 10 burgers in the state of Arizona. Actually, also a good excuse to get out of Phoenix summer's 115 degrees to Flagstaff's cool mountain air, 30 degrees cooler at 7,200 feet elevation.

Now, Angelina pushes her plate aside and pulls her cup of jasmine tea closer to her. She places both hands face down on either side of her teacup and seems to sit up a little straighter as if she is about to make an important presentation. Guy tries unsuccessfully to hide the smile that spreads across his face. He finds her concentration both amusing and charming.

She says, "For starters, would you agree that sometimes crimes are solved in a serendipitous manner?"

"Well …," he hesitates. "Not quite sure what you mean by that."

"I mean it's serendipity when the very thing you are looking for — perhaps a clue or missing evidence sometimes appears in some form *exactly* when you need it." Her eyes are wide. "But not exactly where you expected it would come from."

"Okay, you've got my attention. Tell me more, Miss Marple."

Angelina says, "See, that's the very thing I'm talking about. There's currently a lot of buzz right now on TV about Agatha Christie. I've watched two documentaries on her life this past week and one movie. The movie is fiction, but ties in with the documentaries so beautifully. For example, in the movie she disappears for 11 days, which is exactly what happened in her real life." As Angelina speaks, her pace increases with her excitement for the subject. When she pauses a minute to take a sip of tea, Guy feels he can get a word in.

"And this is relevant because …?"

She looks at him as if it should be obvious. "Relevant because what Agatha was the master of, as the documentaries prove, was providing the reader with a twist. And sometimes more than one. The murderer is never the person you suspect it will be. For example, did you see 'Witness for the Prosecution'?"

"Yes, I do recall that one. A classic. Very twisted."

"Exactly. I thought that might be good information for you as you try to solve Esther's death."

"Well, Angelina, as interesting as that theory is, one has to *have* a suspect before they can discount them. It's easy to plant red herrings in a story, but not so much in real life."

"I'd say you have plenty of red herrings regarding Esther."

"How so?"

"There were so many people at the pickleball courts that Friday night. Any one of them could have committed the crime, assuming she was poisoned. I mean, and no disrespect to you, Guy, it doesn't take a rocket scientist to suspect that someone probably poisoned the water she drank between games."

Guy laughs again. "No, it isn't rocket science and we are holding that as evidence, but there is the fact that there must be a motive."

"And that's where the twist comes in." She smiles proudly as if she has already solved the crime.

He says, "Perhaps I could remind you that it's difficult to find the *who* until we uncover the *why*."

"Are they necessarily in that order?"

"No, but trying to figure out a possible motive for each *who* is where the detective work begins … and hopefully ends."

"I know you're interviewing all the people who were there that night. Do you mind if I ask what you are asking them? That's not giving out confidential information, is it? I mean as long as you don't tell me their answers. Or what it is you're writing in that little tattered notebook of yours." She rolls her eyes as a mother might say to a child, "Put on a clean shirt."

Guy doesn't answer immediately but takes his time opening his fortune cookie. He pulls out the little white paper. "Hmm … here's some sage advice."

"Read it to me," she says.

"*Never take advice from a woman.*"

Angelina reaches across and snaps the paper from between his fingers. "Oh, it does not." She reads, "*You will meet a beautiful lady. Take her advice.*"

They both laugh and Guy says, "Guess we are both very creative liars, aren't we? Seriously, Angelina, I love that you take an interest in my cases. And I love brainstorming with you. Really, I do."

"Really?"

"It's just one of the things I love about you." His bluish-grey eyes, now more blue than grey, seem to penetrate hers deeply. She feels her cheeks starting to color and a warmth spreading through her.

She appears to be tongue-tied but then asks quietly, "There are others … ?"

"Many others. And if we ever stop talking about crimes and murder, perhaps we could talk about those instead." He squeezes her hand, which is resting on the table. Then he pulls out his wallet and puts his credit card on the bill as the waitress is passing by and hands it to her.

He rises and says, "I'll be back in a minute," as he heads to the men's room. Angelina sits there feeling both dumfounded and pleased. *There are others?* When he returns, he doesn't bother to sit down but signs the bill and indicates to Angelina that they are leaving.

"Ready?" he asks.

"Yes, but … but I wasn't finished," she says. "There's more serendipity. The poisons. I didn't get to the best part."

Guy slips his arm around her waist. "No, I think the best part of this evening is yet to come."

As they drive home, Angelina is thinking this might be the night they progress beyond a kiss when her amorous thoughts are startled by her cell phone. When Peter's number flashes across her screen, she accepts the call.

"Mom, don't want to alarm you. Sam is okay but he had a little skateboard accident."

"What?" Angelina's heart pace quickens, and she feels a sinking in her stomach.

"He's got a broken wrist and they're fitting him with a cast right now. He thinks it's cool that his friends can write on it."

"Oh my gosh. I'm coming right now. Where are you?"

"We're at Banner Health but no need to come. I just wanted to let you know while I'm waiting here for them to finish.

"Are the girls with you?"

"They were but have gone home now. Leslie had a school project she needs to work on."

"Well, alright, but let me know when you get home, and we can talk further."

When she explains to Guy what happened, he says, "Would you feel better if you saw that he was okay."

"Peter said 'No', but I really would like to see Sam. And keep Peter company in the waiting room."

"Let's swing by," Guy says and at the next light he makes a U-turn. "I have something in my glove compartment Sam might like. Junior detective that he seems to want to be."

While they are stopped at a red light, there is a young couple in the small truck next to them and she is sitting very close to the driver. Obviously ignoring the seat-belt rule. Angelina says, "Remember, before seatbelts and bucket seats, how we sat close to whoever was our crush at the time?"

"Yeah, reminds me of a story. A wife who saw that said to her husband, 'How come we don't sit like that anymore?' He said, "I'm not the one who moved."

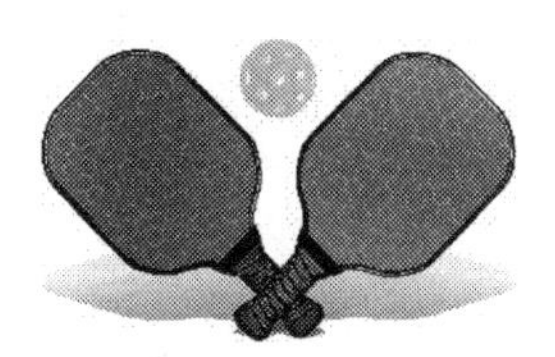

When they arrive in the emergency room, they find Peter in the waiting room, holding a Styrofoam cup of coffee and looking at this cell phone in the other hand. As they approach his chair, he looks up.

"Mom, you didn't need to come." He rises to greet her.

Guy says, "Hope you don't mind. I could tell she wanted to be with you."

"Actually, I'm glad to see you. This is taking longer than I thought. Can I get you a cup of the worst tasting coffee ever?" He lifts his cup as a nurse approaches.

"Sam is ready to go. Follow me," says the nurse.

They find Sam sitting on the examining table admiring his new cast. His eyes open wide when he sees Angelina and Guy. "Grandma, look at this," he says proudly. "All my friends can sign it. They even gave me some markers." He displays a handful. "Do you want to sign it?"

"Of course, I do. But only if you promise me you'll be more careful next time."

Sam looks sheepish but makes no promise. He offers a pen to Guy. "I bet no other kid has a detective signing his cast. This is so cool. Make sure you say Detective by your name." Then after a stern look from his dad, he adds, "Please."

Guy signs and then reaches into his pocket. "I brought you something to help you solve night crimes." He pulls out a little black flashlight. "It helps with night vision."

Sam is elated. "Wow, I'm going to check it out tonight."

Peter says, "And what else are you going to do? Perhaps say *thank you*?"

"Oh sure, thank you." He's already testing the on and off button.

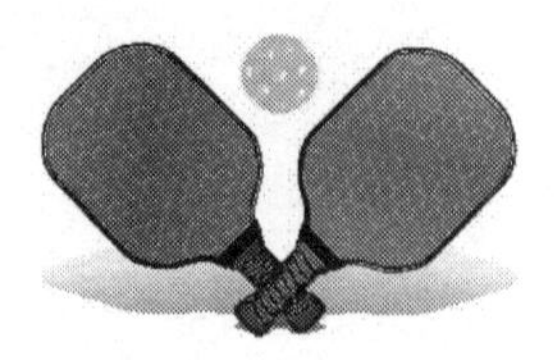

By the time they return home, it's quite late and the promise of *something better* Guy made to Angelina earlier seems irrelevant now. In spite of the late hour, she asks, "Would you like to come in?"

"I think not. Enough excitement for one night."

Angelina is a little disappointed but also relieved as her thoughts have turned to the *what if*, grateful that Sam was wearing his helmet. Guy walks her to the door, and they hug good-night.

"La prossima volta, bella donna."

"Oh?"

"*Next time, my lovely lady*. A little plot twist in our evening. And don't forget that you're the one who says twists are what make for a great story." He brushes a lock of hair from her forehead and kisses her gently on the mouth.

Before she falls asleep that night, Angelina reflects on her evening. Guy's kindness to Sam reminds her of what she heard once. *You can judge a person's character by how they treat children and old people.*

Guy definitely treats Sam well. As for old people? Oh no, was that *her* category? She drifts off to sleep thinking of *la prossima volta.*

CHAPTER TWENTY

To play a dink requires anticipation. It requires patience. It's a set up shot.

Angelina discovers that sitting on the sidelines waiting to rotate into a game might be the best use of her time if she is going to help Guy solve this case. Although he claims he doesn't want her help, she feels he can certainly use any information she will provide. She wants to prove to him once again that she can be a useful sidekick. Holmes and Watson. Cagney and Lacey. Della Street and Perry Mason. Diversity being a buzzword today, it doesn't get much more diverse than a Bulgarian and Italian team. Popoff and Lucchino.

She thinks her information will prove valuable because the snippets of conversation she hears can often be more revealing than a question-answer interview Guy might conduct where people tend to be guarded. Miss Marple or Hercule Poirot would certainly agree. One never knows what is valuable but must gather it all and sort it out later.

For example, it might not be necessary to know from bleacher chatter that Gail's new puppy, Major, ate their remote. They found parts of it on the floor and now wonder where the missing piece is. Part of Major's digestive tract by now? Gail thought he got mad when they switched from Animal Planet to Fox News. Perhaps not relevant to Esther's case, but interesting nonetheless.

What might prove more relevant is overhearing Colleen say that she heard Esther and Christine having a discussion that sounded heated and Christine seemed to storm off in a huff. Then from the lady sitting next to Colleen, who Angelina did not know, who said, "Perhaps Esther was giving her some pointers on the game she didn't want to hear. You know some people do just come out here for fun and exercise, win or lose."

Off to her left, two rows above, she hears two men talking, she believes about Mel who is playing on court four in front of them. "Poor guy. I heard they had a Viking cruise planned for this summer. This has to be a tough time for him."

"Yeh, you work all your life for the 'golden' years. Doesn't seem fair to be robbed of them. Especially in such a weird manner. Do you think she really was poisoned?"

"That's what I'm hearing. Maybe he didn't think those years would be so golden after all. You know, it's usually the husband who's guilty. At least in the TV dramas."

"If that's true, he won't have to wait long for someone else to come along. You know the casserole crusade is in full force in this community for the widowers."

"I'd say he'd be a good catch. Looks fit and seems like a nice guy."

"My wife says if she dies first, I'll follow shortly."

"Grief?"

"No, because I'll starve."

"That's why they invented microwaves."

Then as Angelina is about to get up, another snippet catches her attention from two ladies in the row below her. One, an attractive blonde, says "Have you seen that handsome detective working on the case. Rather swarthy. He's been hanging out here quite a bit. Wouldn't mind giving him some clues. Like my phone number for starters." She giggles.

"I've heard he wants to talk to all the pickleball players that were at Friday Night Potluck. Were you there?"

"No, darn it, but I did know Esther. Played with her a few times. I'm sure I could give him some insight. I do know that she took tons of vitamins. Told us once after a game when the rest of us were worn out and she wanted to keep playing."

"Maybe vitamins *and* steroids?" They both try to stifle a little laugh as if it's disrespectful to talk ill of the dead.

Then Blondie says, "Next time I see that detective, I'm going to offer my impressions … and maybe a little more." She smiles.

Angelina leaves the bleacher area, thinking she has heard enough for one day. More than enough. And perhaps it's time to stake a claim on her territory somehow.

BLEACHER CHATTER

"Hey, Tracy, Decided to take up pickleball?"

"No, I'll stick with golf. Just here to watch my husband play his match."

"Who's that?"

"Bubba. With the black and white tennis shoes. The spats."

"Yep, everyone knows Bubba. He's definitely here for a good time."

A male voice says, "Not like some people. Did you hear about JD walking off the court twice last week? In a social round robin. Supposedly for fun!"

"Why?"

"Something about if people weren't going to play by the rules, he wasn't going to play. He said someone's serve was illegal."

"Bring on the Pickleball Police. Handcuffs and all."

"It's not like most players aren't already handcuffed in some way. Arm bands, knee pads, hamstring support. We're like the poster population for seniors who play."

"And look at Steve. An awesome player with an artificial leg. If he doesn't inspire you, nothing will."

CHAPTER TWENTY-ONE

When Guy suggests that they take a little road trip to explore the state, Angelina is very agreeable, especially after hearing Blondie's comment on the pickleball sidelines.

"There's a great feature in Sunday's paper about Tubac. Have you ever been there?" he asks after dinner at her home.

"No, I haven't, but I saw that article too. I think I even saved it." She goes to a basket beside her desk that is piled high with newspaper pages and starts thumbing through them. "These are all the things I think I want to read again or do something with. But usually once a month I go through them and throw them out. Maybe I end up doing one thing out of 20," she says sheepishly, as if she is a real slacker. "And this stack," she points to a basket full of papers, "is for the Phoenix Zoo animals."

"Oh, the animals are reading now?" Guy says.

"No, silly, my friend Andrea volunteers there and says they are in desperate need of newspapers. Uses them for many things, like litter boxes I think. Who knows?"

Guy looks at her to-do stack, "So I'm not the only one with big plans and little action."

"You have an excuse. You still have a job." She comes to his defense.

"You're too kind," he says as he puts his arm around her shoulders while she spreads the paper out on the dining room table. They read parts of the history out loud, and while doing so his hand gently rubs up and down her back, sending little tingles down her spine.

> *Established in 1752 as a Spanish Presidio (fort), Tubac now hosts working artists whose studios surround the former parade grounds. The village remembers this colorful history well at the Tubac Presidio State Historic Park, located in Old Town, where outdoor displays and an excellent museum bring it all to life. No visit to Tubac is complete without a stop at this, Arizona's First State Park.*
>
> *Or plan a stay at The Tubac Golf Resort and Spa, a historic hotel, on what was the Otero Ranch in Santa Cruz County, Arizona. Spanish Colonial architecture. It was opened as a hotel and golf resort in 1959. The golf course was a principal setting for the 1996 film "Tin Cup."*

"I like the sound of a spa," Angelina says.

" 'Tin Cup.' Very funny golf movie," Guy says.

"I think I missed that one," Angelina says.

"We'll have to watch it before we go. It's hilarious," Guy says.

"I don't know a whole lot about golf but Peter played so I tried a few times."

"Well, it's also a nice love story. You know something about that I'm sure," he says as his hand moves up to the base of her neck and he starts to stroke the back of her hair.

Angelina blushes and says, "Well, yes, a little." More tingles.

"I'd like to know more," he says. "Maybe it's time we both started writing a new chapter in our lives."

Angelina inwardly is saying, *Yes, yes.* Outwardly she responds by pointing to a photo with the article. "These casitas do look charming. Look at the beautiful tile."

Guy says, "I'd rather look at you. What do you say? Shall we book a room? Perhaps just one room?"

Angelina looks into his blue eyes and says, "I think I'd like that."

Guy's smile is huge. "Really?"

Angelina laughs. "Really. But no promises of …."

"Of what …?"

"I don't know. Of anything. Let's just play it by ear and see how it goes."

"Fair enough. I'll make all the arrangements. Let me get my calendar." He pulls his tattered notebook out of his back pocket.

"That's your calendar?" she asks with skepticism.

"Yep, call me old-fashioned but I'm still a paper and pencil guy."

"Guess I'm old-fashioned too." She walks to her desk and brings an 11x14 calendar to the table. "I've tried putting things in my phone but then I can't remember where I put them. Was it in Notes, was it in Outlook? Guess we are a couple of old fogies."

They pick the following weekend to tie in with the art festival Tubac is known for.

Guy says, "I better call now before they get all booked up. I think there's another big hotel in Tubac but doesn't look nearly as charming. Too much concrete."

With their travel plans finalized, Angelina finds her anticipation growing with each passing day. Plenty of anticipation but also some anxiety. Should she shop for a new wardrobe? New nightwear? Or do they call it loungewear now? How long has it been since she's worn a pretty nightgown or something besides an old but comfy tee-shirt to bed?

She has her overnight bag packed two days ahead of time. It is bulging because she can't decide what is appropriate bed wear and wants to be prepared for whatever.

The Friday before they are to leave on Saturday morning, Guy calls and says he'd like to swing by for a minute.

He sounds tense and Angelina asks, "Is everything all right?"

He hesitates and says, "Yes and no. See you in ten."

When he arrives, he gives her a big hug as soon as she opens the door and says, "I am so sorry. We're going to have to postpone our little get-a-way. I'm so disappointed."

"What's happening? "she asks.

"My sister, Sophia, in Chicago. She called in tears. She found out her husband has been having an affair and she's devastated. Said she just had to get away. Away from my mother and two other sisters who are all giving her conflicting advice. Could she come and spend a few days with me. I couldn't refuse her."

"And you shouldn't have. My goodness, we can go another time. I think it's wonderful that she wants to be with her big brother."

"Little brother, actually. Remember, I was the accidental baby after three girls."

"That's right. Three girls who spoiled you rotten as I recall you saying," Angelina smiles. "I think it's time you spoiled your sister this weekend."

"I'm so sorry to leave you high and dry," he says as he pulls her into a hug.

As good as his hug feels, Angelina steps back and says, "April's been wanting to go on a shopping junket. Maybe she's free this weekend. And I can get back to my Agatha Christie poison research that I'm sure you'll find invaluable at some point in your investigation." She gives Guy a smug smile.

As Guy prepares to leave, he says, "You know, I was really

looking forward to our weekend. Exploring Tubac … exploring us …"

Angelina blushes and then says, "Say, why don't you keep the reservation and take your sister. It would be great for the two of you to get away to a nice setting. Make it a special time for both of you."

"Really? That's a great idea. You wouldn't mind?"

"Silly, of course not. Then when we go together you can show me all around. You might, however, want to change the reservation to double beds."

Guy envelops her in another big hug and whispers in her ear, "My dear Angelina. He holds on for a long time and she makes no effort to let go either. When he does let go, he tilts her chin and kisses her softly. "*Sei una donna molto speciale,* very special, that's what you are."

When Guy leaves, Angelina starts to unpack her overnight bag but decides to just keep it intact for the trip they will take in the future. And a future with Guy seems more promising than ever.

CHAPTER TWENTY-TWO

One more important thing to do before he leaves town. Guy gives Mel a call to return the journals.

"Were you able to determine anything from the water bottle or the journals?" Mel asks.

"We're not able to remove fingerprints from fabric, especially this yarn that covered her bottle. Although Scotland labs are making some progress on getting prints off of fabric, it's not available to us yet. And there were no prints on the water bottle, which is interesting. Not even Esther's. That tells us someone wiped the bottle down. Which of course indicates that the poison was probably put into the water bottle. I need to keep it but I'm returning her bag." Guy sets Esther's bag on a nearby end table. "Do you recall how many games Esther played before she fell that night?"

Mel scrunches up his eyes as if he is trying to think hard or perhaps re-live the night in action. "Boy, that's hard to say. I didn't play with her at all that evening. She was playing mainly with the women on court four and I was on court two, if I remember. No maybe court three. But at any rate, I don't know how many games she might have played."

"Do you remember what time you got there Friday night?"

"Round robin starts at four o'clock. We usually play for an hour and then have our potluck about five and those who want to keep playing after can do so. I would imagine we got there about

3:30 and I think Esther got into a game right away to warm up for the round robin."

"Do you know if she made it a habit to drink water after each game?"

"She usually did. She was pretty fanatical about staying hydrated. Often drank those fancy flavored vitamin waters instead of plain water."

"The 911 call was made at 4:47. If she fell at about 4:45, how many games would you say she played before that?"

"Hmm … games take about 15 minutes. Sometimes less. Rarely more. I guess she could have played four or five matches. So I guess that many drinks from her bottle. Was there any water left in the one you took?"

"Just a trace. Of course, someone could have spilled the rest out while she was being administered to on the court. So much commotion, I imagine that no one would have noticed. But there was residue of the poison in the bottle."

"Do they know what poison was used?"

"Nembutal. It's a common sleeping aid but can kill in large doses. It's a common drug for committing suicide because it is painless and works quickly. And often used by vets for animal euthanasia." Guy notices that Mel's right eye starts twitching.

He continues, "It is, of course, prescribed only in small doses. However, someone could save their pills to amass a lethal dosage. Also comes in a liquid form that would make it easier to be completely absorbed in a water solution."

He observes more twitching. Mel rubs his eye but doesn't say anything.

Guy continues, "Thanks to modern technology, we can zero in on prescriptions. There's an electronic data base. PDMP. A prescription drug monitoring program that tracks controlled substance prescriptions in a state. And Nembutal is a controlled substance. The pharmacist told me the data entered is very specific. Who prescribed it, name of patient, even an address and phone number. We're waiting on that report now."

Mel rubs his eye again and when he looks up his expression appears fearful.

"We will find the person, Mel. It won't bring Esther back but we will find whoever did this. Criminals are usually careless in some aspect."

As Guy is going out the door, he turns back to Mel and says, "By the way, I checked with your friends Hank and Betty. They drove your golf cart home and brought both your bags with them."

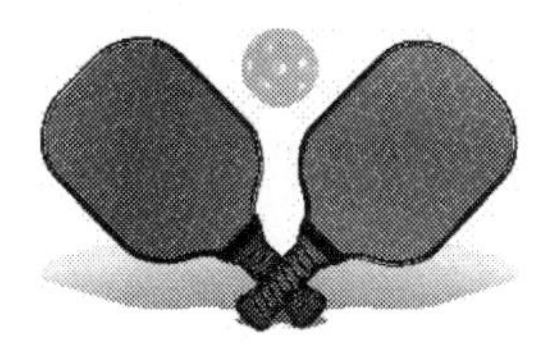

When Guy leaves, Mel goes to his medicine cabinet to check his supply of Nembutal. He wonders if technology can trace orders bought in Mexico. He empties an aspirin bottle into the toilet and puts his remaining Nembutal capsules in the aspirin bottle. He goes to the garage and gets a hammer to smash the Nembutal prescription bottle and dumps the pieces in the trash can, glad that garbage pick-up is the next day;.

Mel fears that if nationwide technology is as efficient as Guy says it is, he might discover that he did have a few prescriptions filled in Kansas. But once they moved to Arizona, Mel, like so many seniors, discovered he could get drugs so much cheaper in Mexico. It was only a few hours hour drive to Nogales and many seniors went there for medications, eyeglasses and dental work at tremendous savings. There was even a monthly shuttle available for those who didn't want to take their cars across the border. When they took the shuttle, they walked through at the border crossing. Upon leaving they were asked if they had bought anything, and Mel always declared the drugs for fear he would be caught in a lie and jailed for life. He saw *Breaking Bad* and a

Mexican prison wasn't someplace he wanted to rot in. But he doesn't recall that they ever wrote anything down so he thinks, *surely no record.*

Mel decides he'll take his chances and not mention the Nembutal.

CHAPTER TWENTY-THREE

Guy calls Angelina as soon as he drops Sophia off at the airport Sunday night. "I was hoping you could meet Sophia but we barely made it back to Phoenix in time for her flight."

Angelina says, "Probably another time would be better anyway. I'm sure she was not up to being sociable. I hope it went well."

"As well as it could. Can't wait to tell you about Tubac." He pauses.

She starts to say, "Can't wait to hear —" when he interrupts.

"I missed you *bella donna*. Can I swing by for a bit?"

"I'd love that," she says. When she hits 'end call' on her phone, she looks around the living room and quickly gathers up the stack of Agatha Christie novels strewn everywhere. She arranges them neatly on the coffee table, which she clears of the snacks she was munching on while reading.

She coaxes fat cat Henry to get off a pile of note papers and stuffs them into a desk drawer. She puts her wine glass in the dishwasher, but then decides to set out two clean glasses. Perhaps a nightcap? She checks the frig to see if there is a bottle of wine chilling.

She rushes to her bathroom vanity where she applies a touch of blush, eyeshadow, and mascara, and a dab of perfume. Runs a brush through her naturally curly hair thankful that she washed it this morning. Looks at the comfortable sweatpants she has worn all day and goes into her closet for something more suitable. And perhaps slightly suggestive?

She opens the overnight bag she had packed for the Tubac weekend and pulls out one of the lounge outfits she bought. To perhaps look like she relaxes at home in elegant loungewear. She pictures a 1940s movie. Lauren Bacall. Sprawled out on a sofa smoking a cigarette with a long, jeweled cigarette holder.

She feels giddy at the prospect of seeing Guy. She thinks that since their recent romantic efforts have been twice thwarted, with Sam's broken wrist and Sophia's broken heart, perhaps third time is a charm.

Charm she thinks and goes to her jewelry box and threads through it until she finds a small bracelet with only two small charms on it — a heart and a cross. It was given to her by Myra after her Peter passed. Dear Myra, who said in the note that accompanied it, *I hope God finds it in his heart to heal yours and bring more love in your life.* Angelina has a wistful smile thinking how ironic that Myra's death was the very reason she might find a new love. Without Myra's investigation, she never would have met Guy.

She is fastening the clasp on the bracelet as she glances in her vanity mirror and realizes that suggestive lounge wear is not appropriate. *What was she thinking? He's spent an entire weekend consoling his sister and is probably quite spent emotionally.*

She hears the doorbell ring and quickly grabs her shabby well-worn robe and throws it on over her silky pink loungewear. *So much for suggestive with this ratty thing on.* She goes to answer the door.

When Guy sees her in her bathrobe, he begins to apologize. "I'm sorry. Is it too late? Were you in bed?"

Angelina shakes her head and then covers her face with both hands and actually starts to laugh. "Don't even ask," she says. When she raises her hands the charm bracelet becomes visible.

Guy says, "Do you always sleep with jewelry?"

Angelina takes him by the hand and pulls him in. "I'm not sleeping and no, I don't sleep with jewelry. It's a long story I'll save for another time. Come tell me about Sophia. And Tubac." She leads him into the kitchen and nods toward the wine glasses. "Would you like one?"

"I would."

As they sip their wine, he says, "I can't wait to take you to this beautiful restaurant in Tubac. *Elvira's.* The setting is magical. It's small and intimate. They have shimmering crystal lights hanging from the ceiling. You feel like you're in a magic cavern. All glittery and romantic. Made this guy wish he was there with someone besides his sister."

"It must be something special for you to talk about the setting more than the food."

"Oh, the food." Guy closes his eyes in a dreamy pose. "Authentic Mexican. The restaurant was started in 1927 in Mexico, and recently relocated just across the border in Tubac. The story is that their business in Mexico was suffering when people were afraid to cross the border with all the cartels. We may have to spend more than a weekend there as I found out there are 10 other restaurants in the area. You know I have a serious obligation to test them all.

"And here's another crazy thing. The golf course rents cows. Real cows to graze on the course so it has a pastural feel. And the bar has a dedication to the infamous 15th hole where Kevin Costner hit his ball 100 times or something like that." When Angelina has a puzzled look, he explains, "From the movie, 'Tin Cup.'"

"Oh yes, 'Tin Cup'", she replies, thinking how charming he looks as he shares his excitement about the place.

They talk for almost an hour and all that time Angelina notices how tender his voice is when he speaks of Sophia. There is no mistake that he loves his sister. And no mistake that she is falling in love with him.

CHAPTER TWENTY-FOUR

When Guy gets the National Drug Monitoring Program report, it reveals a long list of names that had Nembutal prescriptions. Some were listed by the generic name of phenobarbital.

Guy scans the list carefully and doesn't recognize any names until one jumps out at him: Mel Connor.

Guy dials Mel's number. "I'm sorry to bother you again, Mel, but I need to ask you a few questions. Is this a good time to stop by?"

When he arrives, Mel leads him into the kitchen, and they sit. Guy gets right to the point. "I'm rather puzzled as to why you didn't mention that you had a prescription for Nembutal filled when we discussed the poison that was identified in Esther's toxicity report."

Mel looks away and then back at Guy. He admits, "I did get a prescription for some sleeping aids when we moved here. I'm not even sure what the drug was. I thought my doctor said he was prescribing phenobarbital."

"Yes, that's a common generic name for it. Do you still have the bottle it came in?"

"No, I finished that, but I was thinking about getting another prescription. Haven't been sleeping well since … well, since all this has happened."

"I understand," Guy says. Then he confesses, "I myself was

relying a bit on Ambien when Monica passed, but it scared me that I was getting too dependent on it. Heard such horror stories of people who got up in the night doing weird things they didn't remember the next day."

Mel just nods and says, "I heard that too. Something about raiding the refrigerator at night."

Guy chuckles. "Yes, if I'm going to pig out I would like to have some memory of it." He's joking with hopes it will help Mel relax.

Mel leans back in his chair and folds his arms across his chest. Guy mirrors Mel's position, as he's learned through the years often results in making a suspect feel comfortable and more forthcoming with information.

Guy asks, "So did you have trouble sleeping even before Esther passed?"

Now Mel fidgets with the coffee cup he was drinking when Guy arrived. "Can I get you a cup?" he asks as if he just remembers that he has one and has not offered anything to Guy.

"I could use one, thanks."

While Mel goes to the Keurig, Guy pulls out his tattered notebook, thinking he's going to need it.

When they are both settled at the table, Mel looks at Guy and says, "Actually, Detective, I have not been sleeping well for some time. Actually, started in Kansas." Guy doesn't say anything but waits patiently for Mel to continue.

"It's not something I talk about. It's in the past and I want to leave it there but it won't ever leave me, no matter where I live. Hard to forget when you've killed someone."

CHAPTER TWENTY-FIVE

Mel's statement startles Guy. *Killed someone? Someone besides Esther?*

Mel says, "I don't even know where to begin." He runs his hand through his hair.

Guy says, "I'm in no hurry." He leans back in his chair and reaches for his coffee. Mel sets his own cup down with a big sigh.

"I guess it begins with my retirement. I worked for Collier School Bus Manufacturers for 30 years. Good company. In Hutchinson, Kansas. I liked my job but when they offered early retirement buy-out, I thought, why not? Esther had retired as a teacher and we always wanted to travel." Then he shakes his head and looks down. When he looks up, he says, "We had a Viking cruise planned for September."

"I've heard they're very nice. Where were you going?" Guy wants to encourage Mel to relax and keep talking.

"Oh, what does it matter now where? And I'm getting ahead of myself." He lets out a big breath. "So I retire and we take some little road trips and do some things we never had time for when working. Movies in the afternoon, leisurely lunches at some new restaurants in the surrounding towns, joined a fitness club, things like that. Played some golf but honestly, I think both Esther and I got a little bored. She missed being around kids — didn't miss the lesson plans and classroom so much with all the changes in education. Said they were so restricted as to what they could do. Had to 'teach to the test,' she said. So she started volunteering in the school library a couple of afternoons a week. One day she came home and said she saw a huge sign on the school bus. 'Drivers needed.'

"I thought, why not? Sounded like the perfect job to me. Three to four hours a day. Weekends, holidays, and summers off. Being around busses my whole life, I thought it would be fun to drive one — maybe one I helped design."

When he pauses for a sip of coffee, Guy says, "Sounds like it was a perfect fit."

Mel smirks, "Perfect." Then a scornful laugh. "Until that March afternoon. A spring storm across the Kansas prairie. Came on suddenly on a day that started perfectly clear. By the time the children were released from school, there was poor visibility and ice had formed on all the roads." Mel stops talking as if he can't go one. Guy waits.

"Driving my normal route taking the children home, I was cautious, barely touching the gas pedal. Hell, I had driven on snowy roads all my life. I crept along and made several drops safely to parents huddled at the stop eager to rescue their child from the storm." Mel looks down and covers his face with his hands. "It haunts me constantly."

Guy doesn't say anything.

"There was only one little girl left on the bus when I tapped the brakes lightly on the curve and it began to skid. I almost panicked but remembered to turn into the skid. I was able to get it back in my lane. It frightened me so much though that I slowed down and pulled off to the side of the road. And stopped. In retrospect of course, with the poor visibility, it was a terrible decision."

He looks up with a pleading look, "I needed that moment to think. *Should I abandon the bus and take the little girl with me and call for help? Perhaps to the police to come in a car with four-wheel drive.* I decided that was the safest thing to do. I was just about to unbuckle my seatbelt and walk back to get Penelope when the truck plowed into the back of the bus.

"My seatbelt was still fastened, but my head hit the steering wheel and it stunned me. For a moment I was dazed and then I heard someone banging on the door. I leaned down and pulled the lever to open it. A man jumped in and said, 'Are you alright. I followed your taillights. I didn't know you had stopped.'"

Then Mel says directly to Guy, "How stupid I was. That's the first rule of pulling off the road in a storm. Turn off your taillights. What was I thinking?

"Then I remembered Penelope. I rushed down the aisle. I found her lying on the floor in the aisle. Her neck was at a weird angle. I was afraid to touch her. She was lying so still. The truck driver had followed me down the aisle and I yelled, 'Call 911. Now. Get help. We need an ambulance.'"

"After that it's a blur and like the rest of the events were in slow motion. A wailing siren. Flashing red lights. The snow still coming down.

"Penelope didn't make it. And I was responsible. Now you know why I can't sleep. I thought I'd never sleep again."

Guy shakes his head in disbelief. "I am so sorry, Mel." He waits patiently for Mel to continue.

"There were no charges. It was ruled an accident, but perhaps I would have been better off in jail. To be punished as I should have been. Hutchinson's not a very big town. We couldn't stay and face people who knew Penelope. Who knew her parents? Hell, Esther had her brother in fifth grade. Thank goodness he wasn't on the bus that day. Rode home with another students' parents after basketball practice.

"When Esther suggested we move to Arizona, I thought it might help. Not to see that road ever again. Or to drive on an icy road. In a way I felt like a coward leaving, but staying would not have brought her back. The only good thing that came out of it, if you could say *anything* was good, was that I was instrumental in getting seat belts installed on our school buses. Something long overdue."

Looking at this broken man, Guy thinks that in spite of the thousands of miles he was able to put between himself and this tragic event, no distance would ever erase the sadness of the tragedy.

Mel goes to the medicine cabinet after Guy leaves. He pulls down the aspirin bottle that contains the remaining Nembutal he has. Only six. Perhaps it's time for another run to Mexico to stock up. Life without Esther doesn't seem worth living. First Penelope and now Esther. Too many losses and some days he feels he just can't go on.

CHAPTER TWENTY-SIX

Remember, someone took you under their wing when you started playing,
so pay it forward and make it a point to play with players who are weaker than you.

Angelina and Clara go to the pickleball court without the guys. Guy is not available, and Frank says he'll go next time when Guy can play. June, of course, tags along although she doesn't intend to play. She'll do her usual, sit in the bleachers and make new friends while passing out Gummy bears. Or annoy others with Bible verses.

"Maybe we can find two other people to play with," Clara says. "I've heard that you put your paddle in the rack and when one group finishes, the next paddles in order can go on the court. Sort of a rotation."

"But what if the people are so much better than us?" Angelina says doubtfully.

Clara says, "Oh, come on now, we're doing fine. We'll never get better if we don't play."

"I think we should sign up for a few lessons, don't you?" Angelina says.

Clara agrees, "It wouldn't hurt. Maybe we can sign up for some. Come on. Where's your adventurous spirit?"

"This is a little different than Mah Jongg, Scrabble, and canasta. For one thing, we're sitting down for those games."

"And lots of snacks," June says, as she pops a green Gummy.

Clara puts her paddle in the slot board attached to the wire fence surrounding the court where four players are in a game. She takes Angelina's paddle and places it in the one next to hers. "See, you get in line and when they're done, the people with the paddles in here get to play next."

"What if there's not four paddles?" Angelina asks.

"Some people stay in. I think the winners stay and losers come out and put their paddles in these slots for the next game."

"How do you know all this Clara?"

"I was watching the other day. It's really a neat system. Seems fair and organized."

"I'm not so sure about this," Angelina says hesitantly. She glances again at the game in progress. "They look like good players."

About that time the game on the court ends and all the players approach the net and click their paddles. "Nice game." "Good game." "Thanks."

The players start to walk off to get their water bottles when Clara says to them, "Guess we're next in line. Can we come in now? We're ready to play."

An attractive lady in a matching purple top and skirt, with a pickleball paddle design on it, looks at Clara as if she has two heads. "Are you 3.5 players?"

"Not sure about that," says Clara. "Not sure what we are."

Purple lady says, "They have rating clinics once a month. You should get rated. You people should play with your own skill level." Then she turns to her three-some. "Rematch?"

The other three follow her back onto the court with no regard to her comments as if she is the Alpha dog.

Angelina feels her face turning red. "Come on Clara, let's check on that lesson." She pulls her paddle out of the slot and nudges Clara to start walking, before she says something else to further embarrass them.

Clara, who seems stunned by the rebuff, says, "You people? Really?" But she retreats, paddle in hand and they turn to leave.

The man in the bleachers near June who has witnessed the exchange says, not too loudly, "Hey, don't get discouraged. There's a lot of nice people who play here. Uh, she isn't exactly one of them." He nods toward the court where Purple People Eater is starting to serve. He goes on, "If it's any consolation, you're not the first one she's offended."

"Thank you," Angelina says.

He adds, "You know we were all beginners at one time. "I know the pro holds a session every Monday morning. Helped me a lot when I started. And I met a lot of nice people." He stands and waves to a man walking toward him. "There's my group. Gotta run."

June follows Clara and Angelina and says, "She wasn't very nice. I heard a lady got poisoned on the court a few weeks ago. Maybe they got the wrong person."

Angelina and Clara both laugh at the thought of June choosing the next victim or even expressing a hateful thought.

"Gummy anyone? June says. Then as they walk to their car, she says, '*Some who are last shall be first.*' That's Luke 13:30 if anyone wants to know."

BLEACHER CHATTER

"I'm dropping out of the ladder play. Too hard to schedule. Always one of the four who can't make it at the designated time. Then there's 20 texts back and forth."

"I think it should be a set time. Play or don't play. If you can't play at that time, you find a sub."

"Jim deserves the purple heart for setting it up and dealing with all the changes each week. He said his wife Marty reminds him of what Abraham Lincoln said, "You can please some of the people all of the time, you can please all of the people some of the time, but you can't please all of the people all of the time."

"Would drive me crazy being in charge of the ladder."

"In your case, it's a short drive," replies someone with a chuckle.

CHAPTER TWENTY-SEVEN

Although Guy is working this case alone, he goes into the station to track down his former partner Bill to brainstorm the Esther Connor case.

"So, what have you got so far?" Bill asks.

"Not a whole lot. Here's what we know." He pulls out a yellow legal pad and draws a line down the middle. In the left-hand column he makes bullet notes.

- Autopsy reveals poison.
- Nembutal, a controlled substance, also often prescribed as phenobarbital.

Guy says, "In moderate doses it's used as a sleeping aid. In larger doses it kills. Often used in suicide because it's quick and supposedly painless. Literally takes a person's breath away. Often the drug of choice for suicide and euthanasia. People with cancer. Mercy killings."

Guy goes on, "The PDMP (prescription drug monitoring program) tracks every prescription filled in the United States. But lucky for us, or maybe not lucky, we're only a few hours from the Mexican border. They call this drug *death in a bottle.* In liquid form it's more potent than even their strongest tequila."

"Don't people have to declare drugs they are leaving Mexico with? Or at least show a prescription?"

"Yes, but how many do? Seems awful risky to not do it. Pretty stiff penalty if caught," Guy says.

Bill says, "They probably show them their bottle full of Viagra, Prilosec, or birth control. Or smile at the crossing guards with their new dental implants."

"If they would stop using the Viagra, they might not need the birth control," Guy says with a chuckle. "And to make matters worse, Nembutal is a drug to euthanize animals so pet supply shops and vet pharmacies are fully stocked. It's right on the shelves." Guy looks at his legal pad. "So we've got the means but suspects are scarce. Or I should say, just the opposite. So many people on the courts that Friday night. Walking by the fence where all the bags are hanging, most of them with water bottles in the side pockets. Or some just leave their bottles on the bleachers. No one pays attention to them. It would be easy to replace a bottle. Except Esther's bottle was very unique and specific to her. Her bottle cover had some of those little sparkly things — whatever they're called."

Bill says, "So someone would have had to plan this well in advance. To get the substance, to know what kind of water bottle she used and find an exact match and to make the switch at a time no one is looking." Bill adds, "And to hope she drinks enough water that night to be lethal. And to not suspect the taste after the first drink?"

Guy says, "Nembutal supposedly has a bitter taste, so probably was mixed with a drink like Gatorade or those popular protein water drinks her husband said she liked. Here's the irony of that. If she took a swig after each game, which her husband said she normally did, instead of hydrating herself, she was signing her own death warrant."

Bill asks, "Wouldn't she have had any symptoms or problems before she finished the whole bottle?"

"You would think so," Guy says.

Bill asks, "So any possible suspects? The husband? Maybe an

affair. Jealous lover lady?"

Guy says, "Husband seems genuinely distraught. I Googled him and only thing that came up was a tragic accident he was involved in. Driving a school bus. Which he confessed to me when I discovered he had a prescription for Nembutal. Sleeping aid after the accident."

"Just one prescription?" Bill asks.

"Two actually. One in Kansas where he drove the bus and one here in Arizona."

"Any trips to Mexico that you know of?"

"No, but I'm going to do a little further digging there."

"So, you got nothing from interviewing the people there that night?"

"Nope. One lady owed Esther money and she was quite defensive about it when I discovered it but doesn't seem like enough. But I can tell you Esther wasn't the most popular person on the court."

CHAPTER TWENTY-EIGHT

Betty makes a list of people to invite to Taco Tuesday at their house. She tries to have different people each week, mainly from the pickleball group.

She says to Hank. "I heard that the detective who was interviewing all of us about Esther is now playing pickleball. I met his lady friend, Angelina, the other day. Seems like a nice lady. Maybe we should include them this week."

Hank nods. "It would be interesting to see if he'll talk about what's going on with the case."

"I doubt he'll discuss it." Betty says as she counts the names on her little notepad.

"You never know. Once someone has a few drinks, maybe a loose tongue."

"And, of course, we want to have Mel over again. See how he's doing." She smiles.

When she phones Mel, he isn't quick enough with an excuse and Betty is not only persistent but perceptive. "Mel, I know you don't feel like socializing yet but I'm going to insist. You know you'll feel better once you get out and mingle with a few people. We're going to have several people over … not just couples … so you won't feel like a fifth wheel. It's not a sit-down formal thing. Just hang out on the patio. Have a few drinks. And my tacos are awesome."

Mel can't figure out how to get out of it, as Betty is surely aware that his social calendar is quite empty, so he relents and shows up.

When he arrives, Hank leads him out to the patio where Betty is stirring up a big pitcher of margaritas. Mel opts for a cold beer and reaches into the cooler for one when he looks up and sees Detective Guy doing the same. They both register a little surprise at seeing each other.

Mel says, "I didn't know you and Hank were friends."

Guy says, "Not really. I mean I met him once. Doing the interviews with people on the court ...." He's about to say *that night* and realizes that would be tactless so quickly adds, "My friend, Angelina and Betty have become acquainted." He's careful not to mention that they also met on the pickleball court.

"Betty does have the reputation for getting people together," Mel says as he walks away.

Guy pops open his can of Michelob and looks for Angelina. She's engrossed in a conversation with a few other women so he saunters over to a group of men standing near the chips and salsa table.

As he reaches for an appetizer plate, he hears one man saying, "I've been getting all my meds in Mexico for years. My eyeglasses too. Can't beat it. Why pay top dollar here?" Having just had the Mexico conversation with his partner Bill, Guy perks up when he hears this and inches closer to the group.

Another man says, "I've saved a couple thousand on dental work. It was good work too. Did you know they even have a shuttle that goes once a month from here? Don't have to worry about driving, parking, any of that. It's a smooth operation."

Guy joins in the conversation as an innocent bystander. "I've heard good things about that. So I'm curious. When you get a prescription filled, do they ask you at the border if you bought any drugs?"

"Oh yeah. Every time. But it's no problem. Just tell them what you got. Not like I'm doing narcotics," he laughs.

One of the men says, "I think it was Hank who told me about Mexico. Said he went down once."

"And the wives insist on getting that pure Mexican vanilla. I think that stuff should be declared a narcotic." They all laugh.

On the way home, Angelina and Guy talk about what a pleasant evening it was and so nice to be included.

"And those tacos were delicious," Guy says.

"Yes, Betty evidently has a reputation for being a great hostess…even though they haven't been here very long. And that's not all. On the way out to the patio, we walked past her craft room and she does some interesting things. She decorates these little flasks for the lady golfers. Maybe I should take up golf. I heard they have little sips of Rum Chata and Firebird as they golf. I think they're called birdie shots. Do guys do that?"

Guy laughs. "No, we just have bragging rights over the beer afterwards."

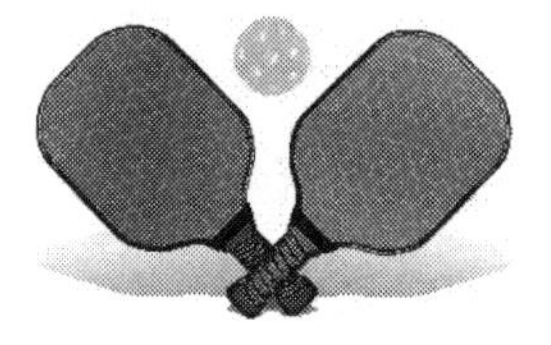

The party ends early like everything else in the retirement community. There are frequent jokes about no cars on the road after 7pm.

As they're cleaning up Hank asks Betty, "So did your detective spill any info? Has he got a suspect or a clue?"

"Not any that I heard of." She wipes dry the margarita pitcher. "This might be one of those perfect unsolved crimes they talk about on a TV series 10 years down the road: The Pickleball Poison."

Hank smiles, "Oh, you're so clever, Betty. So clever." He comes up behind her and puts his arms around her waist. He unties the apron strings she always ties in front and says, "I think this kitchen is clean enough for one night."

CHAPTER TWENTY-NINE

Christine feels remorseful and a bit angry with herself every time she thinks about her conversation with the detective. She shouldn't have gotten so defensive. Isn't that what guilty people do? Perhaps she should call him and apologize. Maybe she should tell him she's going to pay the money back to Mel. That should throw him off her scent.

Then she ponders. Why should she do the very thing she could now totally avoid —repayment and more importantly, her husband Ben finding out about her gambling addiction. No, better to not do anything at all. No payback. No call to the detective. Otherwise, Esther's death would be in vain.

And to confirm that thought, the next evening Ben tells her about a co-worker whose 20-year-old son is in a re-hab center for alcohol and drug abuse.

He says, "The dad is so supportive and forgiving. I feel for the guy. I can't imagine dealing with a loved-one's addition. I mean you love your family and want to help them but, wow, not sure I could do it."

Christine says, "It would be hard," all the while thinking how hard it would have been had Esther told Ben as she threatened to do.

CHAPTER THIRTY

Angelina and Guy are going out to lunch at one of Guy's Food Channel finds. He's quite excited that the show "Restaurant Impossible" has chosen a restaurant close to home, The Ginger Monkey, to revitalize.

As soon as they enter, they realize it's a sports bar with huge TV screens on every wall and a variety of games on display. Soccer, baseball, golf, tennis. There's also two large outdoor patios and the hostess tells them there is live music on the weekends.

It's a Thursday afternoon and not very busy. "I bet it's packed in here on the football weekends. But we're here for the food," Guy says he reaches for a menu. "I checked it out online and, oh boy, it's going to be hard to decide. We're going to have to try a variety I'm afraid."

Angelina looks at her menu. "The only thing I'm afraid of is that if I keep hanging out with you, I'm going to need a new wardrobe. One size larger."

'Remember what you told me a few months ago? When I was hesitant to do the line dancing with you."

"Hmm … not exactly. Refresh my memory."

"YOLO." He says.

She laughs. "True, You only live once. So the teens say, but at this rate that *once* is going to be shortened with high cholesterol surging through my arteries."

When the waitress comes, Angelina says, "Go ahead and order

for us. I'm game for whatever." Guy orders a variety of appetizers to share. It seems he goes on and on.

The waitress says, "So is someone else is joining you?" as if they can't possibly eat all that food.

"Nope, just us. Hard to decide with so many choices. It's our first time here."

The waitress smiles and says, "You picked some of the favorites. Maybe next time you want to try our Monkey Burger. It comes with a special bacon onion jam."

Guy looks at Angelina as if he's asking her permission to add on, but she says, "I think *next* time is a good suggestion." The waitress leaves.

"So tell me about this "Restaurant Impossible" show. I'm assuming it's from your favorite Food Channel."

"Of course. This guy, Robert Irvine, takes restaurants that are failing, about to close their doors and comes in with a new business plan, sometimes a new menu and sometimes even a total remodel. And suddenly they're profitable. And then they're featured on his show. Talk about great advertising."

He goes on, "I have a plan too. Like those guys that are baseball fanatics and their goal in life is to visit every baseball stadium in the country. Sometimes with their kids, which is kinda cool. Well, I have a goal too."

"Wait, don't tell me," Angelina says. Every Restaurant Impossible?"

"*Non sei solo bello, sei intelligente.* You're not only beautiful, but smart."

"It isn't rocket science when it comes to you and food. But don't get me wrong. I love being your sidekick in this adventure."

Guy says, "Oh, and one more very important food stop. When the State Fair comes to town this fall, we have to go and have fair food. All things fried. Fry-bread, fried Snickers. Surely our cholesterol can handle one fry-fest a year?"

Angelina says, "I have great memories of the little carnival that came to our town each summer. Less than a block from my house. We watched them assemble the rides, then went every night, as much as our money would allow, which wasn't much, and then sadly we watched them tear it down."

"I heard that the Ferris wheel at the Arizona State Fair is one of the largest in the U.S. It's called the Big Wheel. 400 feet! And talk about putting a ride together. I think assembly takes 20 hours."

"Well, you're not getting me on that," Angelina assures him.

"We have to go. After dark. And when it stops at the very top, that's when you kiss your best girl."

She smiles, "Perhaps I could be swayed. As long as you don't rock the boat like my brother always did."

Their food arrives — several platters. Angelina says "I don't even know where to begin. It all looks delicious."

"I'm starting with the Twisted Ribs. My taste buds are twisting at the looks of them." Guy reaches for one and takes a bite of the juicy morsel.

"Delizioso," he says as he wipes his mouth with his napkin and takes another bite.

Angelina starts with the Bruschetta Medley. Four breads with a variety of toppings. Goat cheese, Marscarpone, brie, prosciutto, and fig jam._"So good."

Between bites she says, "You know, Guy, speaking of twists, we never had a chance to finish our conversation about the Agatha Christie mysteries."

"Oh yeah, something about the many twists."

"Yes, many twists, many poisons and one other thing that seems to occur in many of her stories."

"Go on," he says as he reaches for the Bacon Jalapeno Popper Chicken bite. "I'm listening."

"It seems that so many of her cases are solved when she discovers something unusual the murder victim and the killer have in common. Some little thing no one else is aware of. Remember, I called it serendipity. I don't know if that's the right word, but I like saying it."

"That makes sense. Finding that missing common element I guess is what good detective work is all about."

"Or sometimes, just plain snooping. For instance, do you know what Esther's hobbies were — besides pickleball that is?"

"Can't say that I do. Very perceptive, my dear Angelina. I will make note of that and see what I can find." He reaches for a slice of bruschetta.

"I could help you. Now that I am getting to know some of the other ladies who play pickleball."

"You know any information is always welcome. But please, Angelina, don't put yourself in harm's way … again."

CHAPTER THIRTY-ONE

When Guy returns home, he checks his phone for any messages and sees that he has missed a call from Mel.

The voice mail says, "Uh, Guy, I think I need to tell you something else. It might be important. Give me a call."

It's rather late but Guy calls Mel. "You said there was something else?"

"Yes, but probably best if I show you. Can you come over?"

"Now?"

"If you can."

Guy leaves immediately and when he arrives, Mel leads him into the kitchen where he has several sheets of white paper laid out on the counter. The papers show fold lines in thirds to fit the number ten envelopes beside each one. Envelopes addressed to him personally at their Kansas home with no return address but a postmark from a town in Kansas, Colwich.

"I don't know why I didn't tell you about this sooner but like I said, I try to put everything about the bus accident out of my mind. Even though that's not really working."

Guy looks at the papers. Ordinary 8 ½ by 11 white sheets with what looks like the font a typewriter would make on each one. *You stole a child's life.* The next one said, *How do you sleep at night?* Next was *You'll pay for this.*

Mel says, "So when we came to Arizona for a get-a-way after the incident and found several nice homes for sale in this wonderful retirement community, Esther suggested we just move here. I had to agree that we needed to get away. And then just before we moved, there was one more note. *You can run but you can't hide.*

"After we had been here several months and there were no longer any notes, we began to relax a bit, thinking we had done the right thing to move. We thought the threats were over. Whoever was writing them perhaps didn't know where we had gone. At least that's what we hoped. Or they had come to terms with their anger.

"We didn't think they were from Penelope's parents as they didn't seem to blame me. I was so guilt-ridden I thought about offering them a large sum of money but Esther said that might insult them. As if money could replace their daughter.

"We threw ourselves into all the community activities here to try and put the past behind us. Pickleball proved to be one of our favorites. Nice people, new friends and a great way to exercise.

"And then Esther's death. I wondered if someone had found us and wanted revenge. But it didn't make sense and I guess that's why I didn't tell you sooner. Why would someone kill Esther if I was the one driving the bus?"

CHAPTER THIRTY-TWO

After an early dinner at her townhome, Guy and Angelina have coffee on her patio. The scent of citrus blossoms waft through the evening air which is in the low 70s. They are surrounded by pots of pink and white petunias, red geraniums, yellow snap dragons, and purple pansies. There's a small section with a raised garden of tomato plants, lettuce and herbs.

Guy sighs. "This is one of those nights when everything seems so perfect. The temperature, the colors, even the coffee tastes better."

"It is the magic hour, you know," Angelina says.

"No, I didn't know."

"In Denmark, that's what they call the last hour before sunset and the first hour before sunrise. The lighting is softer and transitional."

"Have you been there?" he asks.

"No, I just read about this the other day. Denmark scores highest on the happiness index and they attribute that to something called Hoo-ga. I think that's how it's pronounced but it's spelled real weird: H-y-g-g-a. That entire language seems to be mainly consonants. Anyway, this Hoo-ga has to do with lighting and candles in their homes. Even in their workplace. How it creates the perfect atmosphere."

"As dark as it is there in the winters, I can appreciate their love of candles. As for happiness?"

"This article described Hoo-ga more as a sense of comfort, togetherness, well-being."

"Well, that's definitely how I'm feeling now. But I think your peanut-butter brownies might have more to do with it than the lighting." He pats his mid-section.

"It is a perfect Arizona evening but I often miss the change of seasons. Growing up in the Midwest like we both did, don't you?"

"Don't miss shoveling the snow or scraping an icy windshield on a cold Chicago morning. We didn't have a garage."

"We didn't have a car." She laughs. "Sounds like we're trying to outdo each other on how deprived our childhoods were."

Guy says, "Yeah, the old walked-10-miles-to-school, uphill-both-ways stories. You want to talk hardships. I had to share one bathroom with three sisters. A miracle I ever got to school on time."

Angelina says, "My dad took the bus to the foundry each day. My mother walked to the corner grocery several times a week since our freezer was only big enough to hold two ice cube trays." She smiles. "Funny thing. We had so few material things but I never felt deprived, did you?"

"Never. Except maybe when some of the other guys had brand name tennis shoes my family couldn't afford on a fireman's salary. Most of the kids in my neighborhood were in the same boat. At least I didn't have to wear hand-me-downs with no older brothers. And I did get a new blue bike. Great memories of that Schwinn."

Angelina looks toward her small, raised garden of herbs and a few tomato plants. "I have a repeating vivid memory … a good one … of coming home from school on one of those first warm spring days, carrying the jacket you needed in the morning but not at three o'clock. My parents starting to turn over the dirt in the garden space. Everything smelled fresh and I just wanted to stay out in the yard and take it all in. To soak it up. Running in the house to change into maybe the first pair of shorts of the season. Or the day we took the storm windows down and washed windows. That was a sure sign of spring and good weather ahead. There was a wonderful exuberance after a long winter. You just felt lighter. Although as a kid you don't think of it as a great day to be alive, but looking back, that's how it felt."

Guy says, "I think I know what you mean. Like you want to ride your bike and not hold onto the handlebars. 'Look, Ma No hands!' That feeling of freedom and soaring."

Angelina says, "My parents had a large garden, none of this small, raised box of herbs." She glances at her tiny garden. "They got down into the real soil. I can see the rows of plants but it was mostly only two types. Tomatoes and peppers. Banana peppers, which by the way, I have yet to find in Arizona. We canned jars and jars of tomatoes. I can picture the clean glass Bell jars on white towels waiting to be filled. Sometimes I think when we have this lovely weather all year long, we miss those rites of passage each season. Are there things you miss about the Midwest?"

"I miss the sound of a Sunday. Or I should say the lack of sound. Sundays were quiet. You knew it was a Sunday just by stepping outdoors. Didn't need a calendar. And there were the church bells. So many ethnic neighborhoods and each one had its own church with their bells pealing out on a Sunday morning."

"Yes, it was the same in my neighborhood. A beautiful sound. I also miss the fireflies on a summer night. Catching them in mason jars. My goodness, I am getting so melancholy," she says apologetically.

"No need to feel bad about that. I guess we're at an age where we have time to reflect. And remember those good memories." Guy smiles at her kindly. Tonight, his eyes in the twilight are more grey than blue. He says, "It's hard to believe we grew up about 30 miles from each other and now we meet, 1,500 miles away and years later. I wish I knew you as a teenager. I bet you were so cute."

"Oh, no doubt about it," Angelina rolls her eyes. "Actually, I wasn't. If I was, I didn't know it. Kinda chubby, wore glasses thick as Coke bottles, and those were the days when the saying was, *Men don't make passes at girls who wear glasses*. I believed it. I finally got contacts in my thirties. And then recently cataract surgery so back to twenty-twenty vision. Amazing."

Guy laughs, "Well, I'm glad I know you now. And for the record, you look very good to me." He raises his coffee cup to her in a salute. "And your little oasis here…sort of a sanctuary. Very peaceful."

"I guess it is a sanctuary of sorts. Some of Peter's ashes are here in that urn." Angelina points to a deep azure blue pot. "Although he never lived in this house, I know he would have loved it here. I downsized a few years ago. The patio faces east, and he was definitely a morning person." She sighs. "Do you have Monica's ashes … or was she buried?"

"She's buried here at Memorial Gardens. I used to go often but not so much anymore. Every time my daughter visits, we go together. Brings her mother up to date on what's going on in her life. It's very healing for both of us."

Angelina wants to say something comforting but before she can, he adds, "Seeing your beautiful flowers reminds me that I should go soon and plant some. Would you consider going with me? You seem to have a green thumb."

"I'd be honored to go. You told me Monica was sick for quite a while. Did you talk about what your life might be like if she passed before you?"

"We did. And she gave me permission to re-marry. In fact, she insisted that eventually I find someone — to not be alone."

"Peter was the same way. But at the time I couldn't even imagine another relationship at my age, let alone a husband." Then she adds in a perky tone, "Did you know that Agatha Christie's second husband was an archeologist?"

"No … and what made you think of that now?"

"Oh, I guess the second husband discussion. I read somewhere that an archeologist was the best husband a girl could have."

"Because …?"

"Because the older you get, the more interested he is in you."

Guy laughs and says, "Angelina, you are obsessed with Agatha."

"I am. Wish I could get inside her fascinating mind. She would have this Esther thing solved for sure. But I'm working on it. Might have something for you yet."

"Oh really? How's that?"

"I'm going to visit Betty. I heard that she and Esther were friends and hope I can find out what Esther's interests were, besides pickleball that is. Looking for that common thread that Agatha says reveals so much."

"As I said earlier, go ahead and indulge your curiosity. Just be careful, okay?"

CHAPTER THIRTY-THREE

Angelina pulls out her black-and-white speckled notebook and makes some notes. At the top of the page she writes, *Esther Hobbies or Interests*. Now that she's meeting the other ladies who play pickleball, it might be easier for her to discover these hobbies than Guy ever could. It was so nice of Betty to invite them for tacos and seeing the craft room gives her just the excuse she needs to call her.

"Betty, thank you again for inviting us to taco night. Everything was delicious. And so nice to meet other people."

"I like to cook and entertain. Nothing fancy. Just good ol' Midwestern hospitality."

"I saw your craft room. Do you do any classes at your home?"

"Oh, gosh no. The clubhouse does offer a variety of them if you're interested. You know, ceramics, quilting, watercolors."

"I was particularly curious about those little golf flasks you decorated. I'd like to buy one for my daughter-in-law. She's a golfer." *Just a little white lie*. "I'm sure she'd love it. Do you have some already made or could you customize one with her favorite colors?"

"I suppose I could make one for her. Why don't you swing by and I can show you some designs?"

"Would you? That would be great."

Angelina is excited that she is once again in pursuit of clues and can't wait to impress Guy if she discovers anything new about Esther.

When she arrives, Betty leads her to the craft room with shelves of ribbon, colored papers, a long work bench with a glue gun and a paper cutter on one side. There is a sectioned tray full of decorative ornaments, bling, bling, as she calls it. Little colored jewels and even some tiny sparkly letters of the alphabet.

Betty reaches up on a shelf and pulls down two little flasks, one in turquoise and one in red. "Would your daughter, or is it daughter-in-law, like either of these colors?"

"Daughter-in-law. Erica. I think she'd love that one." Angelina points. "She wears a lot of blues."

Betty pulls out a drawer containing more little pieces of decor. "I have some little miniature golf clubs and golf balls. Would this be good?" She holds up a tiny sparkly golf club.

"Oh, perfect, but I'll leave all that to you. And no hurry. Whenever you have time." Angelina looks around the room again before they walk out. "This is the perfect room for a little craft party. Sure you wouldn't consider an evening of instruction if I got a few of my friends together? Maybe just two or three of us?"

"I might consider that. If it was just one night. I wouldn't want to commit to anything long-term. Hank and I still like to travel, sometimes on the spur of the moment."

"That's the beauty of retirement, isn't it? And more time with friends. By the way, I wanted to express my sympathy for the loss of Esther. I was told you were friends."

"Yes, we were." Betty answers somewhat curtly as if she doesn't want to discuss it.

Angelina feels a pang of disappointment, sensing she's not going to get the information she hoped for. All she's going to get is a flask. A turquoise flask with golf balls for a daughter-in-law who doesn't even play golf.

"Can I pay you now?" Angelina reaches into her purse.

"No, just pay me when I'm done."

As they leave the craft room, Angelina points to another shelf where a few metallic water bottles are displayed. "Do you do water bottles also?"

"Oh yes, they're very popular. As you know, everybody has one. We can't drink enough water in the desert."

"Have you made any for the pickleball ladies? I bet those would be very hot sellers."

Betty replies rather briskly, "I told you I just do this for fun. Not into sales."

"Well, in that case, I really do appreciate your doing the flask. Erica will love it. Always trying to keep a good relationship with my daughter-in-law. Do you have children?"

"I have a son and daughter."

"How nice. Here in Arizona?"

"No, they're not." Betty looks at her watch and Angelina feels she may have worn out here welcome.

"Thanks again. Just call me when it's ready."

"Will do," Betty says as she walks Angelina to the front door.

Angelina sits in her car for a minute, the black-speckled notebook on the seat beside her. She picks it up and starts to write before she forgets her train of thought. *That didn't go as planned. No info on Esther. Betty not as friendly as she was at her party. Maybe she needs a sip of Margaritas to open up? And most people love to talk about their children. Not her. Perhaps not a good relationship with the son or daughter. And why didn't she mention where they live if not here. That's what people normally do. Most people go on and on ad nauseum about their kids and grandkids.* She sets the book back on the passenger seat, starts the car and then pauses. She opens the notebook again. *Makes water bottle designs. Maybe not a wasted trip after all.*

When Betty calls Angelina to say the flask is ready, Angelina says she'll swing by. She'd still like to find out something about Esther if possible. Or perhaps who Betty made any water bottles for. Keep digging.

But Betty replies “I’m out and about. Give me your address and I can drop it off today if you’re home.”

CHAPTER THIRTY-FOUR

"I think we should have a game night with some of the pickleball people," Angelina says to Guy.

"Night-time pickle? Are there lights on the court?"

"I mean at my house. Like board games or dice games. Or charades."

"That sounds like fun. Who were you thinking of inviting?"

"Well, that's where I need your input. Probably eight to twelve people. Two or three card tables. Or one big table for left-right-center."

"I may not be much help. Love to play games, but not really up on them. Been years."

"I mean help with the guest list. I want to include anyone you think might be a suspect in Esther's case."

"What?" Guy lets out a laugh.Angelina says, "Yes, you know how Agatha Christie always gets all the suspects in one room. Like in *Then There Were None.* Well, not only a room but an island. No escaping. And, of course, the classic *The Mousetrap*, longest running mystery play on Broadway ever. All in one house. Or because it's England, it's a manor." Angelina assumes a snooty pose and raises her pinkie as if drinking tea.

Guy says, "If my memory serves me correctly, I think some of those suspects are also murdered in their *trapped* locations. Are you planning a poison party, my dear little sleuth?"

"That's it. You've helped me already. Let's have one of those mystery dinner parties. I think the whole thing comes in a box … all the characters, the plot, everything. Oh, this is good."

"Hold on, Agatha. I don't have any suspect lists for you."

"Okay, we'll start with the usual. The husband, Mel. And we need to reciprocate with Hank and Betty, and let's have that nice couple who we met on the court last week from Chicago. I'll buy the mystery game and see how many characters we need. Hopefully I can find one where poison is involved. Oh, this is going to be fun."

"You can't invite Mel if the death is by poison. Or by any means. That wouldn't be appropriate."

"You're so right. What was I thinking?"

Guy says, "I love your enthusiasm but what do you hope to accomplish?"

"Well, that's going to be *your* job. Observe. Who acts nervous at the thought of poison? Or murder. Or just looks suspicious."

Guy laughs. "Whatever. I agree it could be fun. As for finding the killer, I'm sorry to discount your theory but I am quite doubtful. Especially if the only people you invite are your friends."

"Just humor me," she says.

"Long as you don't poison my tea now that you're turning all British on me."

She says, "Reminds me of that famous Winston Churchill quote which is escaping me now. Something about poison."

Guy says, "Oh, yes, Lady Astor says to Churchill, 'If I were married to you, I would poison your tea.' And he says, 'If I were married to you, I would drink it.'"

They both laugh and she says, "Since we're not married, I guess you're safe."

BLEACHER CHATTER

"Can't play this week. I've got frozen shoulder. So I said, 'Doc, explain to me how, when we live through these Arizona summers at 115 degrees, someone can get a frozen shoulder.'"

"Drives me crazy to play with Patsy. She cannot keep the score or server straight. And she's been playing over a year. It's so distracting."

"Keeping score is definitely the hardest part of the game."

Big Rich: "My wife asked me to take her somewhere she's never been."

Little Rich: "So where did you go?"

Big Rich: "I took her to the kitchen."

CHAPTER THIRTY-FIVE

Guy and Angelina are having brunch at a seafood restaurant a friend recommended, High Tide, in Gilbert. When they order Bloody Mary's, the waiter asks them if they want theirs with shrimp and bacon. Guy is ecstatic. "Guess we don't need to order an appetizer." While sipping their Bloody Mary's, they look at other couples and play their observation game.

Angelina says, "Let's check out your skills, Detective. Don't stare, but that couple at the table across from us. The lady wearing the green sweater. Married, dating, or brother/sister?"

Guy glances over and observes the middle-aged couple. "I'm withholding judgement for a minute. Let's see what they do when their food arrives." When the waitress sets down two plates for the couple, Guy observes and shortly after he says to Angelina, "Married. A long time."

"And you say that because …."

"The minute their plates were set down, without speaking a word, they started trading, or sharing, whatever you want to call it. She gave him a large portion of her fries and he passed her his broccoli. Obviously, they know what the other one likes. They didn't even have to ask."

"Very good," Angelina says. "You know almost every day I'm touched by the affection I see among older couples here. Going past my house on the walking path holding hands, or a wife walking slowly beside her husband while he shuffles with a walker. The other day at the Fitness Center I saw a man help his wife put her feet into the foot pedals on the stationary bike and set her controls. When I commented to them as I walked by that it was so nice to have a helper, she beamed and said, 'Oh, this is nothing, he's also great with nail polish since I can no longer reach my toes.'"

Guy says, "No substitute for many long years together. Someone who knows you so well. Perhaps it's why you hear of so many widowed couples connecting on Facebook from high school. Or meeting again at a class reunion. There's something to be said for knowing someone in their early years."

Angelina sighs. "You're so right. A shared history…especially during the teen angst years. I don't know how it is for you, but I miss that comfort that comes from knowing someone so well you often don't even have to say anything. They just know."

"I do too." he admits. Then, "Well, since that's not an option for us at this stage in our lives, I guess the next best thing is to try to fill in some of the gaps?"

"Like favorite color or favorite food?"

"I was thinking of something a little more in depth. Like what's one of the most embarrassing things you've done?" he asks.

"Oh my, we'll be here all evening. It's quite the laundry list."

"Good excuse to order a dessert." Guy picks up the menu.

"Like you need an excuse." Angelina laughs.

"See, you do know me already."

She says, "Well, one comes quickly to mind because I've told this story so many times. It was early in my marriage. Peter's company won an all-expense paid trip to Acapulco. I mean *all* expenses. We could not spend a dime, other than if we wanted to tip someone. There were about 30 of us from different branch offices and parts of the country. Each morning they would give us a list of activities we could choose from to enjoy like deep-sea fishing, golf, local sightseeing. One day Peter chose golf. I barely knew how to play but did enjoy being outdoors. They sent a cab for us, a Volkswagen bus that took us to this elegant course. I think it was called the Princess.

"They rented clubs and all the accessories, and the van actually waited there for us while we golfed to take us back to the hotel. Where, of course, there was an all-expense dinner waiting for us with the other couples. You get the picture? After three days of decadent spoiling, it was time to pack up. They asked us to put our luggage outside our room door early so it could be ready for transport to the airport. Peter went down to the lobby to check out and I finished packing and put the luggage out. Now, it must have been the first very luxurious hotel I had ever stayed in because I was not familiar with how the mini-bar system worked. And because everything, I mean *everything*, on this trip was free, I packed the entire mini bar into our luggage, assuming it was also free."

Guy almost chokes on the sip of coffee he has just taken. "The entire mini bar?"

"Yes. And when I got to the lobby and stood talking to the other wives, Peter was in the check-out line and as each person went to the counter, their tab was very small, like 10 or 20 pesos. Peter's was like 10,000 pesos. He turned in shock and looked at me across the lobby. He said, 'Angelina, did you purchase something from the gift shop?' The clerk then said something about the minibar, and I said, 'No, but I did pack up the mini bar.'"

Guy shakes his head in disbelief.

"By now our luggage was on the way to the airport in the first van and so were the entire contents of our mini bar. I think I still have some of those cute little miniature liquors they stock. Kept them as souvenirs."

Guy says, "That's a good one. See now, I know you so much better. And I'll for sure do the last-minute packing when we leave Tubac."

"So what's your story?" she asks.

"I recall crashing a wedding reception. There's that wedding venue in Chandler. I think it's called Ashley Castle. Well, they actually have two sites with a shared parking lot. I was alone. This was after Monica passed. Had she been there I'm sure this would have never happened. I went into the wrong venue and had a drink at the open bar and helped myself to several appetizers from trays the waiters were walking around with before I saw the bride and groom and realized I didn't know either one. I hightailed it out of there and ran across the parking lot. Not so fast that I spilled my drink, which of course, I took with me."

"Of course, you would take it. See, I guess I do know you."

"It's pretty easy to crash a wedding. Each one assumes you're from the other side."

"Shall we try it sometime? To live on the edge?" Angelina suggests. Then she shifts gears, "Do you know how long Esther and Mel were married?"

"No, but I'm assuming a long time."

"No children?"

"No. And they're fairly new to the community."

"So probably not a lot of friends to comfort and console. We should invite him for dinner."

"That would be nice. I remember all the invitations I had for dinners after Monica passed. I went although I really didn't feel like being around people. As I recall it seemed all their concerns and conversations were frivolous compared to my grief."

"Yes, I remember feeling that way too. But Mel was at Betty and Hanks's Taco Tuesday."

Guy says, "Perhaps he feels some connection with them being from Kansas and all." Then he remembers Mel saying he was trying to put Kansas behind him. Wouldn't Betty and Hank be a sad reminder more than a comfort?

As they leave the restaurant, they both smile at the couple across from them who are enjoying each other's broccoli and fries, proof of a long marriage.

CHAPTER THIRTY-SIX

"I'm so excited about the Mystery Dinner Party. It's called Pasta, Passion and Pistols: Solve a Murder in an Evening with friends," says Angelina.

Guy says, "Wish it were that easy. Too bad it's not Pasta, Pickleball and Poisons. Might give us a clue."

Angelina reads the instructions out loud:

The succulent aroma of home cooked pasta is drifting from New York City's most popular Italian eatery, La Speranza, but something else is heating up the kitchen —cold-blooded murder. Restauranteur Pepi Roni has been shot in the back with his own pistol. Tonight his family and friends will gather to pay their respects to poor Pepi, but one of the guests won't be shedding any tears.

She looks at Guy as if to say, *You get this don't you?* "See, there's our first clue for Esther. Who in the pickleball gang would *not* be sad to see her gone? We have to find that person. Did you attend her Celebration of Life?"

"Yes, I did, not because I knew her well, but to observe of course."

"Anything strike you as unusual?"

"Not really. It was quite well attended so a lot of people to take in." Guy gives her a puzzled expression. "Why do I feel like I'm the one under suspicion here."

"Just want to be sure you're doing your job," Angelina assures him. "Getting back to the game. There's dialogue, between the guests and questioning of each other and it says everyone has to answer questions truthfully. As a player, you try to convince everyone that you are innocent while also trying to determine the murderer's identity. Only the murderer is allowed to lie."

Guy says, "As most murderers do. I took a six-week course strictly on how to detect lies."

"Oh no, I better be careful. Can't get away with anything." Angelina raises her eyebrows as if she is scheming, then asks, "Was it helpful? Useful?"

"I think so. There's a few tricks investigators use. They ask a question they already know the answer to, like where do you live? Have you had lunch? Observe their body language. This tells them how a person normally answers the truth. Then they ask a question that they know is a lie so they see a pattern of how this particular person's body language is when lying. Then they ask the real questions they want to know. And observe."

He goes on, as if he wants to share the entire class with her. "Hands are the richest source of body language. The most revealing. People who lie often try to control their hands, unconsciously, by keeping them still or hiding them behind their back."

Angelina immediately puts both hands behind her back. "I didn't eat that last piece of pie, honest." She laughs. "And for the record," she brings her hands back out, "I love your hands —and that's the truth."

"Really?" Guy looks at his hands, palms up, as if seeing them for the first time.

"Really," Angelina says, "But back to our mystery game, part three is the accusation everyone gets to make. Accusation is based on three questions a detective must answer: motive, who had a reason; means, who had access to murder weapon; and opportunity, who had a chance, as in no alibi."

"Like Colonel Mustard in the ballroom with the wrench?"

"Sort of, but here's the part you'll really love ... the box includes recipes for a complete authentic Italian dinner."

"Mama Mia." Guy throws a kiss to Angelina.

CHAPTER THIRTY-SEVEN

When Betty comes by with the golf flask, Angelina invites her to step in. "I can't wait to see it," she says when Betty hands her the little gift bag.

Angelina opens it and exclaims. "Oh, it's adorable. She'll love it. Let me get my purse." When she returns, she pulls out several bills and asks how much.

Betty replies, "$15. The flask itself was $10," as if to justify the price.

"Oh, $5 is not nearly enough for your beautiful work." She hands Betty a $20.00 and says, "I insist."

Betty says, "Thank you," and turns to leave.

"Wait, if you have a minute. You have such a good eye for decorating. I'm trying to do a wall arrangement out on the patio. Would you step out and take a look at it for me?"

Betty agrees and follows Angelina to her garden sanctuary.

"It's lovely here," Betty says. "Very colorful."

"I'm thinking of this." Angelina points to a patio table where she has displayed a small series of framed bird photos. She points to the wall above the table. "Do you think I should put them in a row or staggered?"

Betty steps back and looks. "I think staggered."

"See, I knew it. When you said you were coming by, I thought, I'm going to ask Betty. Just knew you would have an eye for it. And I made a pot of fresh coffee. Won't you sit a minute out here with me?"

Betty hesitates and then agrees. "It is quite lovely here. Perhaps just a few minutes."

"Great, have a seat and I'll be right back."

When Angelina returns with the tray of coffee and two mugs, Betty is looking at the raised garden. She says, "Hard to grow a good tomato here in the desert. I do miss a Midwestern beef steak tomato from that rich black soil."

"Oh, so do I. Someone said you were from Kansas?"

"Yes."

"Isn't that where Mel and Esther were from? Small world, isn't it? Did you know them before you moved here?"

"Not really. I mean no, we didn't. Mainly our pickleball connection. Here."

"Did Esther have other interests besides pickleball?"

"That I wouldn't know."

For a minute there is an uncomfortable silence and Angelina feels like she has struck out once again in getting any information about Esther.

CHAPTER THIRTY-EIGHT

The night of the mystery party there are eight people gathered in Angelina's living room. Two couples from the pickleball players, including Hank and Betty, June, and another widow friend, Dianne, and Guy and Angelina. They are seated rather closely with small appetizer plates on their laps. They are enjoying the first course of an antipasti platter of roasted red peppers, sautéed mushrooms, salami, and roasted garlic white bean dip. Angelina reads the rules of the game while they munch. When done, she collects their plates and distributes pencils and the individual packets with their scripts and clues. They are dressed in appropriate garb for their character, the most interesting being Father Al Fredo in a priest's cassock, carrying a bottle of red wine (for religious purposes only).

Everyone seems to be in the spirit of the evening and taking their roles quite seriously. Someone jokes that it is not fair that there is a detective in the group as he certainly has an advantage over the rest of them with his deductive skills.

Guy defends himself. "But each case is different. No two the same so I have no advantage here."

Betty says, "Speaking of cases, how's the investigation of Esther's death coming along? I suppose you can't discuss, but are they any closer to finding out who did it?"

Guy says, "You're right. I can't discuss an open investigation."

Hank says, "Maybe no two cases the same, but there must be

similarities in all murder cases, wouldn't you agree? Like motive for instance. Isn't it often jealousy? The jilted lover. Or greed. Who gets the money when the victim dies?"

Angelina says, "I would say revenge is a big one. At least in many of the Agatha Christie's I read."

"And she reads them all. I can vouch for that," Guy says. "And I must say, she is a super sleuth."

"Agatha or Angelina?" Betty asks.

"Both," Guy says. "I have to admit, she did help me solve a murder last year."

Angelina blushes, "It's how we met. But believe me, dating again at my age is the greater mystery to me."

The evening progresses quickly, the murder is solved, delicious pasta is enjoyed and over dessert of spumoni and mocha cake with ricotta cream, everyone agrees it was a fun evening.

When the guests are gone Guy stays. "Let me help you clean up," as he starts to separate dishes and silverware."

She says, "I actually love cleaning up after a party."

"Really?"

"Yes, when guests offer to help, I shoo them out. I like to reflect on the evening and cleaning up is a way to do that and unwind."

"And maybe have that last glass of wine?"

"Of course, no use saving such a little bit in the bottle," she says as she refills both their glasses. When the dishwasher is loaded and the food put away, they sit down for a minute with their wine.

While Angelina and Guy reflect on the evening, so do the others on their way home. One says, "I was sure the murderer was Tara Misu with her big red lips and flirty smile."

The other says, "I thought it was Angel Roni. Killed her own father. Couldn't wait for her inheritance."

June says to Dianne, "I thought it was Clair Voyant. You know hell hath no fury like a woman scorned."

Dianne says, “Is that a Bible verse?”

June says, “Sounds like it should be, but I think it’s Shakespeare.”

Hank says to Betty. “That was fun. Angelina’s a great little hostess.”

Betty replies, “She is also somewhat of a little snoop too. She sure had a lot of personal questions when she came by the house last week. Maybe a few too many.”

CHAPTER THIRTY-NINE

Angelina says, "So, did solving this murder give you any insight into Esther's case?"

Guy ponders a minute. "Not really, but I do like how the game simplified the process. motive, means, opportunity. Sounds easy enough, but of course, it isn't. We need to find that motive first of all."

"We?" Angelina asks in delight. *He's including me now?*

"I wish real murders could be solved in an evening," Guy says.

Angelina senses Guy's frustration and asks if she can be of help. "I know you can't discuss the details of the case but let me help. Maybe just be a sounding board."

Guy looks at her and says with a chuckle. "Sounding boards usually don't talk. I think that might be a challenge for you not to."

For a minute Angelina looks hurt and Guy says quickly, "*Stavo solo scherzando. Just kidding, my dear*. I have been overly cautious to not divulge confidential information but you're right. You are trustworthy and maybe I'm overlooking something very obvious here." He pulls out his tattered notebook.

Angelina quickly goes to her desk and opens a drawer that contains her black and white speckled notebook that she likes to use for her countless lists and projects.

Guy says, "I've done the legal pad thing with my partner, Bill, but let's do it again with you. I know your perspective, as a woman, can be very intuitive. Let's start with motive, as we said at the Mystery Dinner. What are some possible motives?"

She writes *Motives* at the top of the page. Angelina doesn't hesitate. "Okay, the obvious. Greed, money, who would benefit from her death? Was there a life insurance policy and who is the beneficiary? She writes *Money* on the next page.

Guy says, "I've checked that, and her husband is the sole beneficiary of her life insurance policy. Not huge. $100,000."

He goes on, "There is a suspect who shall go unnamed who owes Esther $3,000 but she was repaying her and that hardly seems like enough to murder someone. Although she was very defensive when I questioned her. And she was at the Friday night Pickleball Potluck."

"Let's move on to another common cause: jealousy. Did Mel have a girlfriend? With Esther out of the picture, perhaps a nice life for them with Esther's insurance money?"

"I haven't found any evidence of a girlfriend and Mel seems genuinely devastated. Or else he's an excellent actor."

"Let's think outside the box. What if Esther's death was random? By a serial killer who is going to pick off pickleball players one at a time. Maybe never got picked to play with the others at the grade school playground. He or she starts with the one person that is not the most popular or as we've been told, not the kindest to new players."

Then Angelina laughs, "If that were the case, we'd have to arrest sweet June as a person of interest. She says she was always the last one picked on any team."

Guy says, "I guess we shouldn't rule out anything. In the meantime, just warn everyone to keep an eye on their water bottles."

Angelina says, "Now how about the revenge theory. If that's the reason, we have to find out what Esther did to someone that would cause them to murder her? I can't even find out her hobbies besides pickleball. Her friend Betty was pretty close-mouthed. I'll try to talk to some of the other pickleball ladies."

Guy says, “Mel told me she was active in community projects. Very vocal at town hall meetings in trying to get a new real estate development that would help many seniors with assisted living. Another group is in favor of a mini-Wal-Mart. It’s quite controversial. That’s one avenue I should pursue further.”

CHAPTER FORTY

Guy checks the Town Council meeting schedule and sees that the critical vote is going to be decided at the next meeting. He attends with hopes to identify Esther's opponents to the residential proposal. Who stood to gain the most by the mini-Wal-Mart market being built?

He sits in the back row and listens to the minutes of the last meeting and through many boring items on the agenda. Finally, when it's time to vote on how the designated property should be used, he wonders if, out of respect to the deceased Esther, people would vote in her favor. Perhaps a sympathy vote, a tribute to her efforts.

Esther's replacement, a Larry Meiser, makes a strong appeal to consider the senior citizens who need assisted living housing, stating that their need is greater than providing the community with yet another retail outlet. He closes with " I urge you in voting to do the right thing. What is most important here? Do you want to save a few dollars each time you shop or possibly save lives?

Guy notices that a few suits in the front row squirm a bit in their seats, some turning around, shifting their positions to view the impact Larry's appeal has on the audience.

The spokesperson for the Wal-Mart addition acknowledges Esther's passing and expresses his condolences. Then he cautions the voters to not let her death sway their vote. He stresses the increase in their property values with the addition of a Wal-Mart and the convenience of having it so near. "If we're really thinking about improving the life of seniors, a neighborhood store will keep them from driving farther distances. And in walking distance for many."

The vote is taken and in favor of the Wal-Mart by only three votes.

The gentlemen in the front row clap each other's backs and shake hands.

Guy hangs out at the exit door and as they pass he hears one of them say, "We lucked out there. That Esther would have given a more convincing argument and rounded up more supporting votes."

Another one says almost in a whisper to the man next to him, "Larry asked them to do the right thing. I think *we* did the right thing."

When Guy returns to his car, he makes a note to find out the names of the developers for the Wal-Mart project. Seems far-fetched but as one of his mentors told him early on, "Follow the money."

CHAPTER FORTY-ONE

Mel accepts another dinner invitation from Betty and Hank only because they tell him there will be other people there and he won't feel compelled to keep a conversation going. He can be a passive observer. Although food has little appeal to him these days, one of Betty's home-cooked dinners sounds good. Better than another frozen meal from the microwave. Better than staring at the four walls, watching mindless TV and falling asleep in the recliner. The worst part is that after that little snooze, he is wide awake when he gets into his own bed. His own lonely bed that seems huge without Esther.

How did life become so unbearable? He thought after Kansas nothing could be worse, but this is. Grief compounded. What's the point of going on? No children, no grandchildren. His affairs are in order. He and Esther decided long ago which charities would benefit from their passing if nursing homes hadn't absorbed all their funds. Like it did one of their friends who was in an Alzheimer's care center for over eight years. Mel never dreamed he would envy him. Now he thinks it would be a blessing if he could forget his past life.

The more Mel thinks about it, the more he is convinced that he is making the right decision. Tonight. When he gets home. Now, he dresses for dinner in his favorite plaid shirt, one Esther always liked, and comfortable khaki Dockers.

Before he leaves the house he writes the note, so he won't have second thoughts later. He sets it out on his desk in the den where he has also lined up the remaining capsules of Nembutal, which he will take before he goes to bed. He adds two other painkillers he found in the medicine cabinet that Esther never finished using after her root canal. He'd read somewhere that mixing painkillers was especially lethal. Then he lays out the folder containing his Living Will and Trust. *No use making someone search all his files.*

As he drives to Hank and Betty's home, he feels almost joyful, as if he's a prisoner enjoying his last meal before execution. No, he thinks, joyful would be too strong an emotion. Perhaps peaceful. A resolution he can live with … or rather die with.

CHAPTER FORTY-TWO

When Mel arrives at their home, he is surprised that there are no other cars parked in the driveway, as he thought he was running a bit late, taking time to write his note and all. Hank greets him with his usual bluster and Mel thinks, as he has many times, what a genuinely nice guy Hank is.

Mel says, "Where is everyone? I thought Betty said there would be others."

Hank says, "We invited the Wilsons, Connie and Tom, but they cancelled. Connie got a bug and didn't want to spread it."

Meanwhile Connie, feeling perfectly fine with no bug, is home on her patio, enjoying a steak Tom has just grilled. Oblivious to any invitation that was never extended.

Hank leads Mel to the portable bar and asks, "Your usual? Jack over a little ice?"

Mel says, "The usual," and decides he's going to sip this slowly and enjoy every bit of it.

Hank says, "So did you play pickleball today? See any of the gang?"

Mel says, "No, never left the house. Didn't see a soul. I don't think I've even spoken to anyone in the last few days."

Hank says to Betty, who appears from the kitchen carrying a breadbasket, "Did you hear that, Betty? Mel hasn't spoken to a soul in days. I'm so glad you got him over here. That's not healthy you know, Mel."

Betty smiles, it seems more at Hank than Mel. Their eyes lock and she nods. Then she turns to Mel, "Hope you like spaghetti. Nothing fancy, but I'm told my meatballs are heavenly."

Mel smiles and says, "Smells wonderful," as he thinks to himself, *Heavenly is very appropriate.* Then he wonders, as if for the first time, *Will I even go to heaven? After Penelope?*

Doubt must have shown in his face as Hank asks, "Are you alright?"

Mel snaps out of his reverie and says, "I'm fine." *Think of something to say.* "Just had a little déjà vu moment. Esther also made delicious meatballs."

Betty says, "It's awful how those little reminders pop up out of nowhere. You know, a familiar scent, a song they loved, the mention of their favorite book or movie. You think you're doing better and then the grief sucks you right back in."

Betty speaks with such passion that Mel says, "You're so right That's exactly how it feels. I'm sorry to ask, but did you also lose someone recently?"

Betty places the breadbasket on the table and turns to look at him squarely with what seems like that menacing look that haunted him after the last dinner. "Not recently, although some days it feels like yesterday. The pain and sorrow."

As they are about to sit down, Hank says, "Hey, Mel, before I forget, would you mind signing this petition?" He hands Mel a pen. "We're trying to get the Fitness Center to change their guest fee policy for pickleball players. You know we members pay quite a bit each year to have choice hours for use of the court and then discover many people who aren't even members are out there. If they want to play as a guest, there should be a fee, don't you think?"

"Makes sense to me," Mel says and scribbles his signature at the bottom of the page.

Hank looks at it carefully and sets it aside. "Thanks Mel." He nods his head and smiles at Betty.

The meal is delicious and satisfying and Mel is not as uncomfortable making conversation as he normally is, thinking the Jack helps loosen his tongue. And Hank keeps refreshing his drink. Actually, taking his glass back to the bar and returning with a full glass several times. It goes down smoothly.

CHAPTER FORTY-THREE

The next day when Mel doesn't show up for his ladder play match and doesn't answer any phone calls or texts, his partners are concerned. One of them, Roger, goes to his house and no one answers. He notifies the police who enter through an unlocked window. His body is discovered, laid out nicely on his bed in a plaid shirt and khakis. He's clutching a small,l framed photo of Esther on his chest. There's a note on the bedside table. "I just want to be with Esther. Forever."

The toxicology report indicates poison, once again Nembutal.

What puzzles the police however is that in addition to the bedside note, there was another farewell note on Mel's desk in the den. Beside this note are six identical pills lined up in a row, and two smaller ones. On a piece of crème colored stationery, it's written, *I'm so sorry, Penelope. Forgive me. Please accept this atonement.* There is a folder with an envelope containing a legal document. It is a trust agreement with the sole trustee named as Toby Paxton.

Because Guy is working on Esther's investigation, he is called in.

CHAPTER FORTY-FOUR

Guy is puzzled. Why two suicide notes? And it appears that both signatures are Mel's but Guy takes both notes with him into the forensics lab for a handwriting analysis. The analysis report comes back saying both signatures appear to be the same, but the content of the notes shows some irregularities. One on crème-colored stationery and one on a small generic lined notepad.

"See here," the technician, John, points to the crème-colored stationery. The capital *F* in *Forgive* is different than the capital *F* in *Forever* on the white note. A forward slant in one and not the other. The small *s* in *just* is different than the small *s* in *sorry.*"

Since Roger, one of Mel's foursome that day, was the one who alerted police that something might be wrong when Mel missed their scheduled ladder match, Guy calls him.

"So when did you suspect that something might be amiss?" Guy asks.

Roger says, "When he didn't show up. Mel is quite reliable. Whenever four of us are scheduled to play a match, he's usually the first one to respond. Then I tried texting and calling from the court and when no answer, I suspected something was wrong. Thought maybe he was sick and might need me to go get a prescription."

"So, this would have been Saturday morning?"

"Yes."

"Did he by chance mention any plans he had for Friday or

Friday night?"

"Not that I recall. We normally just confirm time of play and which court we will be on."

"Do you still have the text?" Guy asks.

Roger says, "I doubt it. I usually delete them once I get a response." But he pulls his phone out of his pocket and starts to scroll through the texts.

"No, I don't see it. Oh wait, here it is. Part of the chain that two others answered after Mel." He shows it to Guy who reads simply. "See you Saturday at 10."

Guy shares this information with Angelina who says, "I suppose you've already thought of this crazy possibility. Was Mel planning his suicide but someone committed a murder wanting it to appear as suicide? And beat him to it?"

"Miss Marple, I think you are a genius."

PART TWO

Kansas

March 25, 2015

The school bus tragedy in Hutchinson, Kansas, threw the close-knit community into shock and grief. In addition to the funeral service attended by nearly every family in Penelope's school, they had a candle vigil and memorial set up at the fateful site of the accident. Parents who had children on the bus that day counted their blessings while they poured their hearts out to the Paxton family: Penelope's father Justin, her mother Beth and Penelope's older brother, Toby. The school provided a grief counselor for all the students and offered evening sessions to any of the community who wanted to attend. The town was in mourning.

She couldn't recall when the thought of getting revenge started. At first, she was so grief-stricken she could think of nothing but her loss. Then the anger, the injustice of it consumed her. So not fair, that justice was not sought. Not that it would bring their darling girl back … but still. And then the thought festered and grew like a gangrene, a spreading disease and took hold of her. *Some people don't deserve to live. To enjoy the company of their loved ones when they've robbed others of that pleasure.* Almost unknowingly, but bit by bit, she began to plot.

The grief counselor told her to keep a journal and express her feelings in it. Her sorrow, her anger. Notes to herself to start healing. But soon she found herself composing notes not to herself but to him. Anonymous notes which she didn't sign or send but there was some satisfaction is writing them. *You stole a child's life and all the joy she would have brought us. How do you sleep at night*? Then she thought, why not send them? Why should he sleep at night when she couldn't?

She didn't want her husband to know what she was doing and since they shared a computer, she dug out the old IBM Selectric she could not part with even after they got a computer. She had hoped to teach Penelope how to type on it.

She never told her husband that she began to mail the letters. He wouldn't understand. He missed Penelope too but he was not a vengeful man. As preposterous as it was to her, he seemed sympathetic to him, the bus driver. He even asked her why she blamed only him. How about the truck driver who ran into the bus? Wasn't he also to blame?

She answered that the bus driver was responsible for children. He should never have pulled off the road. He should have turned off his taillights. It was his fault, his alone.

She couldn't understand her husband's thinking. How could he be so forgiving? How could he even say things like, "That poor man. He has to spend the rest of his life with that horrible mistake."

She responded, "So maybe we'd be doing him a favor by helping him end his life early. He wouldn't have to suffer any more."

He looked at her in shock. "What are you saying? Listen to yourself. That won't bring Penelope back. One tragic deed doesn't deserve another. Especially one that wasn't intentional."

She knew then that she had to keep her vengeful thoughts secret, but she didn't want to. She wanted him on her side. Throughout their marriage they accomplished their goals best when both of them were invested. She needed him if she was going to be successful in getting revenge. She didn't know how she would do it, but knew she didn't want to go it alone. She wanted to succeed. She needed to succeed.

Now she had a double mission. One: To get her husband to feel the anger and vengeance she felt. So much so that he would be willing to go along with her plan. Two: Come up with a plan. A foolproof plan. She didn't even have one yet, but she would. First things first. She kept writing and sending the letters to appease herself.

In the meantime, she never missed an opportunity to subtly, and sometimes not so subtly, point out the joyous future they were missing. The special plans they had for their granddaughter. She purposely left a travel brochure laying out from Rhoades Scholar Program announcing their next season of grandparent-grandchild trips. Full-page descriptions of adventures she knew they had talked about doing with Penelope. A dude ranch in Wyoming, a space camp at the NASA center in Alabama, a music camp in the upper peninsula of Michigan in a beautiful wooded setting. She winced as she recalled Penelope's little freckled face getting so excited when they talked about them.

She arranged for her husband to be with her when she drove past a park when she knew there were special events or outings for seven and eight-year-olds. She wanted him to feel her absence so greatly that he would be consumed with anger as she was.

She made sure they were driving around town on the high school's prom night when so many of the young couples were gathered at the favorite gazebo photo spot, commenting that Penelope would have been so lovely in her prom dress. They attended the local high school graduation because one of their best friends had a grandson giving the commencement speech (they could hardly refuse). She tearfully voiced the thought they both surely had — that they would never see their granddaughter in a cap and gown, marching to "Pomp and Circumstance."

As he consoled her, she sensed that he too was beginning to feel the anger and resentment she had all along. Perhaps her plan was working. And when one day she finally saw the anger in his eyes and the steely resolution she was looking for, she knew she might indeed have a partner and accomplice in her mission. It happened one Sunday.

When they drove the 42 miles to Hutchinson from Wichita, as they did each weekend to visit their grandson Toby, she insisted on driving so she could go past *his* house. Perhaps to get a glimpse of *him* but she got more than she expected.

One, there was a "For Sale" sign in his front yard. Two, he was in his driveway, talking to a young man who appeared to be leaving, as he was opening a car door in the driveway. He slapped him on the back and they both laughed. She slowed down and pulled to the curb across from the house and observed. *He* was laughing. Laughing. How could *he* laugh when their hearts were breaking? And then he hugged the young man. Who was he? She knew *he* didn't have children but why should he be hugging someone, anyone, when they would never have the joy of hugging their granddaughter again? She looked at her husband and he too seemed affected by this demonstration of pleasure. Hugs and laughter. Scarce in their lives these days.

"Perhaps you're right," he said to her. "How can he laugh when all we can do is cry?"

She said, "And the coward sells his house. I bet he's leaving this town. Does the damage and leaves the rest of the community to grieve. Not even man enough to face the consequences."

She continued to send the spiteful hateful letters but didn't know if they were delivered, as she obviously never put a return address on them. She took the time and effort to drive the 18 miles to the nearby town of Colwich so the postmark would not show that they were from Wichita.

Each Sunday when they drove to Hutchinson to console their daughter and son-in-law they would drive past *his* house and then one week, there was a sold sign on the front lawn. Where was he going and how could she find out without drawing any suspicion to herself?

She wrote down the name and number of the realtor displayed

on the "Sold" sign. Perhaps she would have a forwarding address for them but would she reveal it? How to get it?

Utility companies needed a forwarding address for final bills but doubtful they would give that to anyone either. Perhaps the best route was through his friends. She had her work cut out for her.

She never disclosed any of her revengeful thoughts to her daughter. She wanted them to remain innocent. Like her father, Beth didn't seem to hold the driver accountable for the tragedy. She found great solace in her Bible study group as they changed their focus each week since the accident to scriptures and verses that would be most helpful to Beth. Suffering and forgiveness. They gave Beth a plaque that now hangs above her kitchen desk. *The only thing that counts is faith expressing itself through love. Galatians 5:6*

She needed to spend some time in Hutchinson. Time to see where *he* spent his days, who were his friends and acquaintances. She told her husband she wanted to spend a week with Beth, to help divert some of her grief into a therapeutic project. Perhaps going to the fabric store and choosing a new quilt pattern they could work on together as they often did in the past. Beth was happy to have her mother's company even if it was only evenings as she still worked full-time. With her grandson, Toby, in school and Beth and Justin working, it left her time to scope out his routine and hopefully meet someone who would innocently be willing to share his future plans.

Each morning after her family left for work and school, she went to his house and parked across the street, in what she hoped was an inconspicuous location, waiting for him to come out. She discovered he had an early morning routine of meeting with three other men at a coffee shop. After the first day, he returned home and never left the house again. The second day he went to Home Depot after coffee and then the grocery store. He didn't go out again but for several hours worked in his garage as she was able to observe with the garage door open. He seemed to be packing a lot of boxes and stacking them against one wall. Around noon his wife came out with a tray with what must have been lunch. They sat in two lawn chairs in the driveway and ate and talked. How she wished she could hear what they were saying. Perhaps talking about their new location.

The third day she went into the coffee shop shortly after he did and sat in the booth next to the four men, ordered coffee and listened intently to their conversation, hoping it would give her a clue. Then she heard it. "Arizona." *What about it? What were they saying?*

One man said, "I can't blame you. If I had a chance to leave these winters, even for a few months, I would jump on it."

Then he said, "I guess the smart thing would be to go there for a few months, rent something, and see if we like it before we sell the whole kit and caboodle, but Esther's determined. She says she's doing it for me. Says I need the change but she's not fooling me. I know she's as eager to get out of here as I am."

One of the other men said, "Can't blame her. Or you for that matter. The accident has been tough on both of you, and no one would think less of you for trying to put it behind you and start over." No one said anything for a minute, and she was afraid she wasn't going to get any more information.

Then he spoke but not very loudly. His head was bent, and she was straining to hear. It was as if he were talking into his coffee cup. "I'll never put it behind me, but maybe it will help. Change of scenery, not wondering if each person I see at the grocery store or hardware is judging me. Blaming me."

Then one of the burly guys says, "And we'll have a great place to visit. Get us a tee time as soon as you can." This broke the tension and they laughed.

He said, "With 296 days of sunshine each year, I think we can manage that. I do hope you all come to visit. I'd welcome that."

And then, the very thing she was hoping for. One of them said,

"No wonder every place you hear about has the name Sun in it. What's the name of the one you're going to? Sun City, Sun Valley?"

He said, "Sun Lakes."

She quickly took a little notebook out of her purse and wrote it down for fear that in her excitement she would leave there and forget it.

One of the men said, "Guys, I gotta' run. See you tomorrow." The rest of them also stood, left money on the table and walked out.

She sat there, pleased that she had a clue. Now she had to dig deeper. Where was this Sun Lakes and how big was it?

She was so deep in thought that the waitress startled her when she asked if she wanted more coffee, the carafe poised above her cup. "Can I get you anything else?" she asked.

"No, I think I'm good for today." She took out her wallet to leave money for her coffee and said to herself. "I'm really good."

As soon as she returned to Beth's, she got on her computer and googled Sun Lakes, Arizona.

> *Sun Lakes Arizona by Robson Communities is a magnificent 6,683-home community. It is comprised of five country club style neighborhoods that each have their own golf course and amenity center. A generous assortment of world-class amenities and social activities cater to the non-golfers who reside in this age-restricted community. Sun Lakes Arizona is in a great location on the south side of Chandler just 24 miles from downtown Phoenix. The community is conveniently located within minutes to I-10 and the 202 loop. Gilbert, Mesa and many popular shopping outlets in Chandler are a short drive from the community.*
>
> *In each of the five community sections, there is a clubhouse that includes Fitness Centers, restaurants,*

> *hobby rooms, swimming pools and ballrooms. The grounds are joined together by miles of walking and biking trails, scenic parks, fishing lakes, bocce ball courts and tennis courts. For golf-lovers there are five world-class golf courses in each of the neighborhoods.*
>
> *Regardless of where you live in this community, you can expect to have an assortment of enjoyable amenities at your fingertips every day. The newer neighborhoods tend to have clubhouses with updated amenities.*

She sat back in her chair and took a deep breath. *Over 6,000 homes*. She had to narrow it down. She only had one day left of her visit. She went to the coffee shop again the following morning.

The next morning did not prove fruitful. All the men spoke of was golf and their ailments. Something about a rotator cuff and how long it takes to heal. She thought to herself. *Healing a rotator cuff is nothing compared to the healing I'm seeking*. How she wished a surgery or physical therapy could heal a broken heart.

When she returned to Wichita after her week-long visit, she wasn't sure what to do next. Now, she wouldn't even have an address to send the letters to. Not that they were doing her any good. Instead of giving her a sense of peace of any kind, it seemed each letter fueled her anger to a higher degree. Where was the justice?

She tried to pour her love onto the remaining grandchild, Toby, each time they went to see him. At age eleven, he was a sweet boy but seemed to favor Hank as they did "boy" things together. Her heart ached with the thought of all the "girl" things she would never do now with Penelope—the shopping for pretty dresses, the tea parties, the Disney princess movies. She doubted there would be other grandchildren as her son, at age 34, didn't even have a girlfriend. She wondered if perhaps he might be gay but she never asked.

Somehow, they got through the holidays of 2015 and Betty vowed that she would try to make 2016 a better year. But the resentment did not leave her. Instead, it festered and grew. She needed to find him.

One night she asked her husband, "Do you remember how we talked about getting out of the cold Kansas winter for a few weeks. Maybe this is a good year to do it."

"I'm up for that," he said. "You know we have friends in Florida we could visit. Last time we went it was a great getaway and broke up the cold months."

"I was thinking maybe go to the Southwest this year. Something different. Like Arizona. I'd love to visit some of those Native American settlements. I've heard they have beautiful turquoise for sale. I could stock up with some gems for my craft projects."

He said, "Great golf too. I think the Johnsons have a winter home there. We could ask them about it."

"Great idea. I'll give Nancy Johnson a call tomorrow." She smiled thinking, *this is a start.*

The following day she met Nancy for coffee and told her that they were thinking about spending a few weeks in Arizona after the holidays. Could Nancy recommend a nice community to check out?

When Nancy told her that they were leaving for Arizona late October and would be delighted to have them visit while they scoped out the area, she was thrilled. Nancy said their winter home was in a wonderful community just outside of Phoenix. When she said it was called Sun Lakes, the very name she had written in her little notebook in the men's coffee shop, she knew that her revenge plan had the blessings of the universe. She was of the belief that there are no co-incidences. *Everything happens for a reason but I'm going to avenge something that should never have happened.*

November 2016

When they landed at Sky Harbor in Phoenix, they rented a car and drove the 14 miles to Wild Horse Pass Resort, just a mere eight miles from the Sun Lakes community. They were in awe of the cloudless blue sky, the mountains and the 68-degree temperature that day. They had left Kansas at nine degrees with a storm predicting four inches of snow arriving that night.

"Guess we are getting out of Dodge just in time," her husband said as they drove to the airport in Wichita to board their flight.

They enjoyed some time in the casino at their hotel, had dinner and went to bed early as their bodies were still on Kansas time and they had gotten up quite early for their flight. Her anticipation was building as she knew she was about to close in on her prey. At least she hoped she would.

The following day, they were invited to the Johnsons. Her husband and Neal were golfing, and Nancy was going to give her a tour of Sun Lakes and take her to lunch at their country club.

Nancy could have worked for the Chamber of Commerce as her enthusiasm for her community was over the top. She showed her the various amenities available from tennis, golf, crafts, woodworking, quilting, water aerobics, dinner clubs, hiking groups, line dancing, the Fitness Center, and a huge pickleball facility.

"You have to try this pickleball. It's amazing exercise and so much fun. And you meet so many nice people. I think you'd love it here. You really should look into getting a place. Neal was a bit skeptical at first but now he says it's the best thing we've ever done."

They went into the lobby of the clubhouse, which had a huge bulletin board.

Nancy said, "And look at these posters of all the tribute concerts like Patsy Cline, Frank Sinatra, Motown. So cheap too. Tickets are like $25. They sell out the same day."

There were several index cards on the bulletin board saying, "Homes For Rent." She wrote down the numbers and planned to call them as soon as they got back to their hotel.

When they returned home, Nancy showed her *The Splas*h, the community newspaper with all the clubs' activities and then she pulled out maps and directories.

"Look at this," Nancy said as she opened what was called the *Source Book*. You can find anything and anybody in here. All the clubs, services, service organizations, and residents are listed not only alphabetically but also by area and even a section showing which state they moved from." Nancy handed her the book, and she couldn't believe her good fortune.

"So it shows who moved here from our home state, Kansas?"

"Yep, just thumb through there. You'll see it." Her heart was racing and her excitement was mounting. She found the Kansas pages and scrolled through the names listed alphabetically. It looked like about a hundred. She didn't find the one she was looking for and felt a stab of disappointment.

"Is this the latest directory?" she asked.

Nancy said, "Not sure, check the cover for the year. They publish one each year. Looking for someone special?"

She was quick to respond, "Oh, no, just curious. I'm so glad you shared all this with me."

Nancy said, "I think it takes a year to get your name in the directory, depending on when you move in. I know we missed the deadline by one month and didn't get in till the following year."

She said, "I can't wait to tell my husband all about it."

"I bet Neal is giving him a big sales pitch. I mean five golf courses? What guy is going to say no to that?"

That proved to be the case, as that evening her husband said he would love to spend a few months there. "Between the amenities and the beautiful weather," he said, "what's not to love about this place?"

That night she called several of the rentals listed and they made an appointment to see two of them the following day. Several were already rented, and no one had removed the index card.

She was so glad she had not told her husband that *he* was possibly moving here. Or at least she thought *he* was. If they discovered it after they moved here, it would just be further justification that their revenge was meant to be. God had placed them *both* here for a reason.

The next day, they found a totally furnished two-bedroom townhome for rent for six months. "Totally" included bed linens, dishes, silverware; as was often the case of the rentals there, all one needed were the clothes on their backs.

That night at the hotel, watching the national news and another storm blasting the Midwest, they thought, why go home? They decided to keep their rental car and stay. She was delighted.

"Maybe Beth and Justin can drive our car out for the holiday and then fly home. It's just perfect. We'll be back in Kansas for the spring thaw and daffodils."

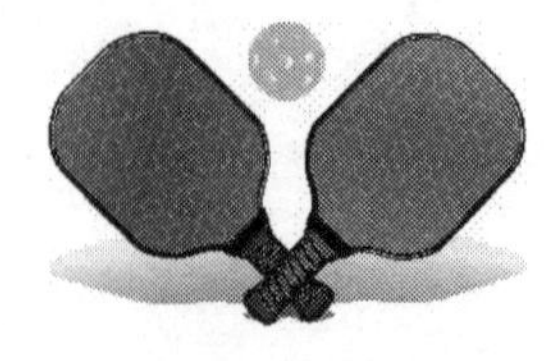

They were officially going to be snowbirds enjoying the best of both worlds. A winter in Arizona, summer in Kansas. Her husband was still unaware of her true motive and had no idea that the school bus driver also lived there.

PART THREE

CHAPTER FORTY-FIVE

It's Saturday date night and Angelina and Guy are of course at a restaurant. Tonight is not a special occasion, but it is somewhat of a splurge. And to make it more interesting, they decide to take the light rail into Midtown Phoenix for Guy's perpetual quest of a unique dining experience.

They enjoy the light rail through Tempe and Mill Avenue in the heart of Arizona State University's campus. "And this way I can have an adult beverage that will wear off before I have to drive us home from the rail station." Guy laughs. "Just trying to keep my record clean."

Tonight is a far stretch from some of the dives Guy has scoured out. They are eating at one of the premier Phoenix restaurants: Durant's. With its 70-year history,1950's ambience, including red leather booths and entrance through the kitchen like gangsters in the Godfather movie, it's a gracious (and pricey) step back in time.

After they are seated, Angelina says, "Maybe you should work for that company that does restaurant reviews. What's it called? Zagat? Then you could get paid for eating." She takes a sip of the signature drink the waiter recommends: the extra dry Belvedere martini with bleu cheese olives.

"Mmm. This is quite good," she says as she admires her fancy martini glass.

"I'm not sure Zagat even has their little maroon book anymore. Probably all online now. Then I'd have to be a tech-y person to submit my review. I think I'll stay anonymous and old-school, just like my drink, which is also excellent." He raises his Old-Fashioned garnished with a slice of orange and cherry. "Very smooth," he says.

They start with fried calamari which is fresh and tender, followed by shrimp bisque. Their main entrée is steak.

"After all, it is Durant's steakhouse. Should be our first clue as to what to order, wouldn't you agree?" Guy asks.

Angelina cuts into her petite filet mignon. She chews slowly and then says, "I definitely agree. So tender I could almost cut with my fork." After a few bites, she puts her steak knife and fork across her plate and sighs.

"You aren't giving up are you?" Guy asks, as he continues to cut into his ribeye.

"No, just taking a little break. And thinking of something that happened many years ago, but I've never forgotten it. It saddens me each time I think of it."

Guy puts his knife and fork down too as if he wants to give her his full attention. "A special memory with Peter?"

Angelina smiles, "No, this goes even farther back. High school." Guy waits. "You know we talked about sharing intimate moments from our past. This one is quite embarrassing, but I'm going to tell it anyway. Enough years have passed."

She takes as sip of her martini as if she needs liquid courage. "I was a senior in high school and dating a sophomore in college. He was from one of the other high schools in my town and we met during the summer at a popular pizza parlor. This one was in his neighborhood, but we girls preferred it to our neighborhood pizza place 'cause we honestly believed the guys at the other school were so much cooler."

"Of course," Guy agrees readily. "We felt that way about the girls at St. Mary's. Especially with their cute plaid jumpers, even though the nuns made them wear them far below their knees." Guy grimaces. "But back to your story."

"I had never dated an upperclassman. I had hardly dated at all actually except for a few special dances that required a date. So I was already a little out of 'my league' so to speak." She takes another sip of her drink.

"At the end of the summer, just before he left for college — he was going to Marquette University on a track scholarship — he said he wanted to take me to special farewell dinner. Up until then we had only gone to the movies and the summer Big Band dances downtown. He picked a fancy steakhouse at the edge of town and borrowed a friend's car. He was the oldest son in a large Hispanic family and although it was never spoken, I sensed that he didn't have a lot of money. I think the money he earned at his summer job he gave to his family.

"When he ordered a steak, I did the same. But when it arrived, I realized it was a big mistake on my part. Here was this huge slab of meat, medium rare no less, and I had no idea what to do with it." She shakes her head with a pitiful smile.

"See, at my home, we ate a lot of stews with small tender chunks of meat. Or lots of loose meats stuffed into cabbage or peppers. Or meatloaf that could be eaten with just a fork. I had never used a steak knife in my life. And sad to say, I didn't start that night. I think I left most of that beautiful steak, that he probably saved for all summer, on my plate.

"Years later I often thought of that night and felt so ashamed that I couldn't accept what he surely meant to be a special gift to me. We wrote to each other that fall but before he came home for Christmas, I had broken up with him, preferring to 'go steady' with one of the senior boys in my class. More in my comfort zone, I guess. No fancy dinners there … just burgers, fries, and pizza. Typical teen fare.

"Even after all these years, as insignificant a blunder as it may seem, I'd give anything to have a chance to explain to him why I couldn't eat the steak and perhaps thank him for treating me so well."

Guy looks at her as if he understands. "Maybe you could find him on Facebook?"

"You know, I thought of that too," she says somewhat sheepishly, as if caught with her hand in the cookie jar. "I have to admit that a few years after Peter died, I did do a search but came up with nothing. Not so much to renew a romance but to sincerely apologize." She looks at Guy with tenderness. "You're very kind to suggest that."

"Yeah, kinda stupid too. What if you found him and there was that spark again?" Guy looks at her longingly. "I would miss you, Angelina, if you found someone else to spend your time with. I really would."

"I have found someone. You silly man." She places her hand on his across the table. On his lovely, long and tan fingers. "Who else would wine and dine me like you do?" She tries to make light of it. "And still care about me after I've gained 20 pounds that are all his fault?" She picks up her steak knife and points it at him.

Guy laughs. "Okay, guilty as charged. But now that you know how to use a steak knife, you can direct it toward the rest of your steak instead of me."

They both continue taking bites of their steaks, when Angelina says, "I don't mean to dwell on this, but you know, the older I get the more I feel the need to atone for my mistakes. To ask forgiveness of those I might have hurt."

"There's more?" he asks, eyes widened.

"Nothing jumps out at me right now, but I'm sure there are several. Perhaps unintentional, but nevertheless. How about you? Need to beg anyone's forgiveness before you get to the Pearly Gates?"

"Surely a few. But what I'm reminded of now is how I've seen convicted killers try so hard to seek forgiveness from their victims' families."

"Do they often get it?"

"In more cases than I would have thought. Interestingly

enough, the spoken act of forgiveness seems to be more healing to the families than the killer."

"I guess it's too late for Esther's killer to ask Mel for forgiveness. But it seems, from his note, he was seeking it from someone."

"Yes, but which note? Are we looking for one killer of both Mel and Esther or two different ones? It's getting complicated and with each passing day, chances lessen. I hope this doesn't turn into a cold case."

"Does it trouble you? Day and night?"

"Pretty much all my waking hours, it's on my mind." Guy looks pensive. Then he brightens, "Hey, let's forget about that for now and order their famous key lime pie. And coffee, since I'm driving home from the train station."

Angelina smiles, "Like, I said, 20 pounds … just a matter of time."

Before she falls asleep that night, she basks in the memory of their enjoyable evening but feels that somehow she has to be a better help to Guy to solve this crime.

CHAPTER FORTY-SIX

Partner communication is important. Call the shot using words like "mine," "yours."
Call out 'bounce it' when you're not sure if the opponent's ball is going to be out.

Angelina is not sure how she can best help Guy but feels she needs to find a way to know more about Esther. Where to begin? Perhaps she can host a lunch for some of the lady pickleball players she has met. She does her best thinking when planning a party, preparing a menu, and cooking some of her favorite dishes. And hopefully some unknown tidbit will be divulged at the lunch. Worst case, she has made new friends.

She decides not to include June and Clara for they never really knew Esther, but she doesn't want to offend them. When Clara tells her that she and Frank are going to Vegas for a weekend, she takes advantage of that time they are out of town. And sweet June need not know of the lunch, although knowing Junie, she would not take offense. She might say something like *There is a time for everything, and a season for every activity under the heaven.* Angelina thinks, If there were only more Junes in the world, I wouldn't have to be helping Guy find a murderer.

She tells Guy she's having some of the pickleball ladies for lunch to get to know them better but doesn't reveal her true intention. He might discourage her, suspecting she is being too snoopy again.

The day of the lunch they gather on her patio after Friday morning pickleball. Eight in all counting herself. Nicole, Christine, Deborah, Betty, Linda, Barb, and Lela.

Angelina is serving her foolproof Quiche Lorraine that she's been making since the 1960s, with an arugula salad of red onions, shaved parmesan, cherry tomatoes, almond slivers (used to be served with pine nuts but currently at $15 a pound she settles for almonds). A simple olive oil and lemon juice dressing, as she discovered on a trip to Tuscany, is the best dressing, with the less-is-more concept. As a side, she serves a crunchy cranberry salad from the grocery deli and buttery bacon and onion scones that she bought frozen from the Hackett House in Tempe, their signature piece. She long ago discovered that she didn't have to do everything from scratch if someone else had already perfected it. And she gives credit where credit is due, not claiming it's her recipe. Also, for fear someone might ask for it.

With a proven menu she has done many times, she can focus her energies on how to get the conversation to turn to Esther without it being morbid or disturbing. They talk about the games they played that morning, how long they had been playing.

Barb says, "I can't understand how one day every serve is good and the next day you can't even get it over the net."

Lela says, "I read somewhere that the net is a good two inches higher at the sides than the middle."

Barb says, "Is that what they mean when they say, middle solves the riddle?"

Nicole says, "I think that refers to hitting the ball down the middle of the court with a good chance each person thinks the other one is getting it."

And then the perfect opportunity presents itself when Nicole comments that she considers herself lucky that the first day she walked on the court, Esther was giving a lesson to Christine and Deborah and invited her to join them.

Angelina says, "I wish I had known Esther. Seems like

everyone had a great deal of respect for her mastery of the game."

"No question about that," Barb says. "Sometimes offensive but we all got used to that. And she was also the first one to compliment you on a good shot."

Angelina says, "Had she been playing longer than most of you?"

Lela said, "I don't think so. I believe she took it up when they moved here. And that wasn't so long ago. Maybe about a year."

Angelina says, "Where did she move from?"

Christine says, "I think Kansas."

Deborah says, "Betty, aren't you also from Kansas? Did you know Esther there?"

Betty says, "No," quickly. Then adds, "I think we came from different cities."

Angelina asks Betty, "What city were you from?"

Betty says, "Wichita."

Deborah says, "I'm from Hutchinson. Isn't that a co-incidence? Three of us from Kansas?"

Betty turns the subject to the menu. "This quiche is delicious. Will you share the recipe?"

Angelina replies, "Of course. It's from the Julia Child's *Mastering the Art of French Cooking*. But I have it in a word doc. Happy to send it out." Several others say, "Oh, I'd like it too," and Angelina now feels she has lost the chance to explore Esther further without making it obvious.

As everyone is leaving and Angelina walks to the door with each of them, she says to Betty. "By the way, my daughter-in-law loves the flask."

Betty says, "That's nice."

"Did I ask if you also decorate water bottles? I was told Esther had a very distinctive one. Wondered if you had done hers."

"I don't believe I did." She answers curtly as she puts her hands behind her back. Then she turns and leaves.

Thinking everyone has left, Angelina closes the front door and sits down on the foyer bench, highly frustrated that the brunch didn't reveal any new information. Then she hears a door open and sees Nicole coming out of her powder room.

She must have looked surprised because Nicole says, "Angelina, are you all right?"

"Oh, yes, I just thought everyone had left."

"I've got so many errands, I thought I should use your restroom before I headed out."

"Truth be told, Nicole, I'm a little disappointed."

"Why? I thought it was a lovely brunch. So nice of you to get us together."

"To be perfectly honest, I had an ulterior motive. Here, come sit a minute." She motions for Nicole to join her on the bench.

"I'm trying to help Detective Guy with Esther's investigation."

"Really?" Nicole seems surprised.

"Oh, not in an official capacity. In fact, he would not want me involved in any way, but I just think if we knew more about Esther's habits and hobbies, it might give us a clue to follow. I was hoping to get some of that information today. Silly of me, wasn't it?"

'Not really. I'm sure if you had asked the ladies, they would have all cooperated."

"Well, I didn't want to be that obvious, I guess. Since I'm fairly new to this group, I don't want the reputation of the batty old lady who thinks she's Miss Marple or Jessica Fletcher."

Nicole laughs. "I see what you mean. Well, I knew Esther fairly well. Maybe I can be of help. And I don't think you're batty. What would you like to know?"

"Do you know of anyone who would have benefitted from her death?"

"Well, it might have been Mel, financially, but obviously, that's not the case now."

"That's what Guy said. Oh, I really shouldn't be discussing this." She waves her hands in front of her as if she can erase that last remark. "But how about hobbies? What did she do besides pickleball?"

"She was on the town council and an advocate for that new senior housing development. I think it's quite controversial, but doesn't seem worth killing someone over it. That's just my opinion of course. As for hobbies, she did beautiful needlepoint. I don't think she took any classes, but I believe she and Betty were talking about doing a project together. Maybe Betty can help you."

"Every time I mention Esther to Betty, she seems to cut me off. Maybe it's too painful. If they were close friends and all."

"I think their project was to make some custom covers for water bottles. I know she made the one that Esther had on her bottle." Nicole looks at her watch. "Wow, I have to leave. I have a haircut appointment. Sorry I wasn't more help. And your secret is safe with me, Miss Marple."

When Nicole leaves, Angelina says to herself, *Oh you did help Nicole. You did.*

Later that evening Angelina confesses to Guy that she tried to find out more about Esther by hosting a brunch of pickleball ladies, but didn't seem to glean any new information.

"Well, there was one bit. Betty and Esther are both from Kansas but didn't know each other there. Not from the same town. But Deborah is from the same town as Esther. That's hardly anything to go on though, is it?"

Guy says, "You never know, but it does seem everyone here is from somewhere else. When I was calling the Friday night potluck list, I've never seen so many different area codes on cell phones."

Angelina doesn't mention to Guy that Betty seems to have lied about Esther's water bottle or else has a very poor memory. Angelina vows to find out which it is.

CHAPTER FORTY-SEVEN

For a good dink shot, you don't need a huge follow-through. Just 'scoop the ball' over the net.

When Clara and Frank return from Las Vegas, they call to set up a pickleball game with Angelina and Guy.

Clara says, "I am so motivated to get better at this game. You won't believe it but there was a national pickleball tournament going on in Vegas right at our hotel. We watched a few matches. Oh my goodness, some of those young players are so good."

"Key word being young," Frank says.

"And we got to meet the number one player now in the nation, Ben Johns. Such a polite young man and quite modest."

Guy says, "Well, as long as we don't have to play against the young 'uns we can surely hold our own with all the seniors here."

Clara says, "But we should get rated. I think they hold clinics for that. I'm going to look into it. Then we can play with people at our level. And maybe break into that elite 3.5 group here that treats us newbies like second-class citizens."

"Oh, that was just one person, Clara," Angelina says.

"There's always one, isn't there?" says Frank. "After watching that tournament, I'm working on the third-shot drop. You wouldn't believe how many volleys the pros have before they score a point and it's mostly those dink shots back and forth in the kitchen."

He and Clara are both wearing their new t-shirts they bought from one of the many vendors at the tournament. His says, Dink

Responsibly and hers says, Retirement, AKA Play Pickleball Every Day.

They play for an hour, switching partners each game.

June watches from the bleachers and overhears two ladies in the row above her talking about their grandchildren.

One says, "I worry so much about them and all those extreme sports they do. I just know one of them is going to crack their head open."

The other says, "I'm a worry-wart too. Seems the older I get the more I worry. About things I really have no control over. Global warming, traffic, cancer. Shouldn't it be the other way around? Like we should have wisdom and peace of mind at our age?"

June can't resist turning around and says, "Phillipians 4-6 *Be anxious for nothing."*

And you know what's really interesting?" She doesn't wait for a reply but speaks quickly for fear they'll get up and leave before she can share one of her favorites. "The phrase 'do not fear' appears 365 times in the bible. I think that's one for every day of the year."

They smile politely at June, but as she suspects, they move over slightly out of her range.

When they all stop in the club for a bite of lunch afterward, another pickleball player approaches their table and addresses Guy. "Is it true?" he asks.

Although Guy suspects what he is referring to, he says, "Is what true?"

"Esther's husband, Mel. Also dead."

Guy says, "I'm sorry to say it is."

"Not another murder, I hope. If so, this sport is getting quite hazardous to our health. Here I was worrying about pulling a hamstring. Maybe I should be worrying about someone pulling a gun." He gives a little chuckle but when no one responds to his sick humor, he says, "So any suspects in Esther's case?"

"Sorry, can't discuss an open investigation," Guy says, and the man walks away.

CHAPTER FORTY-EIGHT

Angelina is determined to find out why Betty lied about making the water bottle cover for Esther, or if indeed she did. Maybe it was an innocent mistake. How to get together with her again without arousing suspicion? She thought she could personally deliver the quiche recipe to her, saying her computer was on the blink, but no guarantee she would invite her in. Sounded like a lame excuse anyway. Washers or dryers are sometimes on the blink. Not a computer so much.

Then a brainstorm, and an honest motive at that. Her women's club was holding a multi-family garage sale to raise money for their scholarship fund. She could ask Betty if she had any items to donate or maybe even make some posters from her craft room for the sale. She gets excited at the prospect and calls her immediately.

Betty says, "Sorry, since we're just renting here I don't have any items. We literally just came with clothes and of course Hank's golf clubs. I don't think he would want me to sell those. She chuckles. "But I'd be happy to make a few signs."

After two days pass Betty calls Angelina to say the signs are ready.

When she pulls up to her house, Betty is in the driveway and the garage door is open. She waves to Angelina to pull into the driveway.

Betty points to a box on the table in the garage. "I did manage to scrape a few things together for your sale. Here's a box of books I've bought and read since I've been here."

"Do you stay through the summer?"Angelina asks.

Betty says, "No, actually we're headed back to our summer home very soon."

"Oh, it seems a little early. Most people wait until May. Have some special occasions at home you're going back for?"

"Not really. But I think our work here is done."

"Your work?" Angelina asks.

Betty looks flustered. "I meant our time. Our playtime. We consider this place a big playground for seniors, don't you?"

"Absolutely." Angelina replies. "By the way, Nicole mentioned the other day you had made some covers for some of the ladies' pickleball water bottles. I thought you were just doing the flasks."

Betty says, "Oh, I can't keep track. I might have done some water bottles too." Then adds in a dismissive tone, "Glad I could help with your scholarship fund."

"Thank you so much," Angelina says as she starts to walk out of the garage. She passes the table with a box of framed photos in it. Angelina notices one of a little girl in a ballet costume. "This is adorable. Granddaughter?" she asks.

Betty says, "Yes, that's our Penelope."

CHAPTER FORTY-NINE

That night at dinner Betty tells Hank about Angelina stopping by.

"She's such a snoop. I can't quite put my finger on it but I always feel like she's probing for information. Too many questions."

"The detective did say at her party that she imagines herself as quite the sleuth, Agatha Christie fan and all."

"You know what happens to those amateur sleuths in most movies, don't you?" Betty asks.

"Often get themselves killed," Hank says as reaches for another piece of Betty's delicious roast chicken.

"I guess at this point, what's one more?" Betty asks.

"One more piece of chicken?" Hank says with a smile, as he holds the chicken in the air with his fork, although he knows perfectly well what Betty is referring to.

"It would take the emphasis off of a family crime motive with Esther and Mel. Now they would be looking for a serial killer. Pickleball players dropping one at a time. After all, the experts highly recommend that drop shot."

CHAPTER FIFTY

Angelina leaves Betty's house mumbling to herself as she drives away. Well, that didn't prove anything. Admits she might have made water bottle covers but I still don't know if she made Esther's other than what Nicole said. So I really don't know any more than I did before. Well, at least got a few books for the sale. Not a total waste of time.

The next day she is pleasantly surprised when Betty calls her and says she has some other items for the sale if she's interested.

"Of course, I am," Angelina says. "What's a good day to stop by?"

"Is Friday too late?" Betty asks.

"No, not at all."

Betty goes on, "In fact, why don't you come for lunch. I'm trying to empty our freezer so I can turn it off before we leave. We'll have a 'mustgo' lunch."

"A what?" Angelina asks.

Betty says, "A mustgo. This food must go."

Angelina laughs and says, "What time?"

Angelina is quite pleased with the invitation and decides she is going to come right out and tell Betty that she's trying to help Guy solve this case and ask what else can Betty tell her about Esther and Mel.

CHAPTER FIFTY-ONE

Guy is immediately in touch with the attorney, Blaine Morris, who wrote up Mel's trust naming Toby Paxton as the trustee, with his parents, Beth and Justin as trustees until Toby turns 21. Grantor is one Mel Connor.

"Have Toby's parents been notified?" Guy asks Blaine.

"I haven't yet. Although Mel did give me their contact information when we established the trust fund."

"Would you mind if I spoke to them before you told them of the trust? I am telling you, confidentially, that it's possible Mel's death was not a suicide. Possibly a murder," Guy reveals to Blaine.

"My goodness, another murder?"

"I can't elaborate now, but it might prove important to my investigation that I speak to the Paxtons before they are aware of the trust. Would you mind sharing their contact information?"

"Anything that might help you. Certainly." He opens the file on his desk, takes a clean piece of stationery with his letterhead and copies information from the folder. He slides it across to Guy. "Keep me posted."

"I'm going to do this quickly and I'll be in touch with you as soon as I do."

As soon as Guy returns home, he books a round-trip ticket to Wichita, Kansas, and a rental car to drive to Hutchinson from the Wichita airport.

CHAPTER FIFTY-TWO

Angelina is looking forward to lunch at Betty's, wondering what other ladies might be joining them. If it's a "must-go" lunch, surely she has enough food to serve many. She wears a soft aqua-colored shell because she has a new scarf with shades of deep turquoise, royal blue and green she would like to wear as an accent along with her turquoise earrings.

When she arrives at Betty's on Friday, she is surprised that there are no other cars in the driveway. She checks the time, thinking perhaps she is too early and can wait in the car a bit. But actually, she's about five minutes late, so she walks up to the door with a small gift bag containing a hostess gift of a scented bar of hand soap.

Betty seems so delighted to see her and seems especially appreciative of the gift, small as it is.

"Will there be any others joining us?" Angelina asks as Betty leads her into the kitchen.

"No, just the three of us. You and I and Hank."

"Oh," Angelina says, trying to disguise her surprise that there would be no other ladies and also that Hank would join them.

'I thought we'd just eat in the kitchen. Seems friendlier," Betty says.

"I totally agree," Angelina says, but now feels quite over-dressed. She removes her scarf and lays it with her purse on a nearby chair.

'I'm experimenting with a new cocktail," Betty says. Have to use up all those lemons, you know. Would you like to try one?"

'Of course," Angelina replies, thinking, *When in Rome* ….

"It's sort of like a limoncello without all the prep time, "Betty says as she hands her a frosted martini glass with a yellow liquid and a sprig of mint and a slice of lemon.

Angelina takes a sip and says, "Mmmmm. This is very refreshing."

Betty says, "I should give it a name. I think I'll call it a Mustgo. The lemons must go too."

Hank says with a smile, "That's very appropriate. Comes a time when everything must go. Food, household items." He sides up to Betty at the counter and whispers out of earshot. "And sometimes people."

When Betty is seated, she says to Angelina. "So how is your day going? Had a busy morning?"

"No, not really. Just doing some reading."

"Something good?"

"Yes. I know it seems silly with so many good books to read that I would read one twice, but it's been years, so it seems fairly new to me. It's *The Murder of Roger Ackroyd* by Agatha Christie. I'm sort of obsessed with her," Angelina says apologetically.

"Your friend, the detective, mentioned that at your Murder Mystery Party, which by the way, was a lot of fun."

"Thank you. Yes, Guy teases me about my obsession. I'm reading this book again because it's murder by poison and since that's the way Esther died, I thought it might give me some insight. I like to brainstorm with Guy about his cases."

"Oh, that's interesting now. Does he discuss them with you?"

"Not really. Confidential information and all that, but we do talk in generalities. Although …," Angelina says, "not bragging, but I did help him solve a murder last year."

"Really? Tell us about that," Betty says.

"Well, it happened to a dear friend of mine, Myra, who I played Mah Jongg with. It just all seemed suspicious to me from the very start. That she was fine one day … passing Mah Jongg tiles to us across the board, joking, and laughing and having lunch … and the next day gone.

Long story, I won't bore you with the details."

"Oh, not at all boring," Betty says. "I doubt that murder ever is. I should have invited Guy to lunch too. I bet he's got some great stories. But I wasn't sure Hank would be joining us until this morning. Thought it would be just us girls. But since he's here, he can put that other box I have for the garage sale in your car. Why don't you give him your keys?"

"Sure." Angelina walks to her purse and fishes out her key fob, which she hands to Hank. "Oh, no problem. Guy's out of town today anyway." Then, in a lower voice as if she's revealing a secret. "I think it has something to do with Mel's death."

Betty and Hank quickly look at each other and Hank says, "Did he happen to say where?"

"No, he didn't. Said he'd call when he got back. We often go to dinner on Friday nights." *And Saturday nights and Sunday nights, but I guess no need to tell that.*

Betty says, "I was thinking of asking a few other ladies today but I thought it would be nice to have you alone. Just to get better acquainted. And then, you know, if you invite one you feel you have to invite another, and it gets totally out of hand."

"I know what you mean. Don't want to leave anyone out."

"Did you by chance mention to anyone that you were coming here?"

Angelina thinks that's an odd question, but simply answers, "No, haven't talked to a soul all morning. Engrossed in that murder I guess."

Angelina hears her phone ringing from inside her purse. She goes to answer and sees an 800 number. She hits decline and says, "I'm turning this off while we have lunch. Seems those telemarketers never let up."

"How's your drink? Can I refresh it?" Betty asks.

“It’s very tasty, but I better go slow. Have to drive home you know.”

“It’s mostly sugar, very low alcohol,” Betty says as she pours a little more into Angelina’s glass.

CHAPTER FIFTY-THREE

Before leaving for Wichita, Guy calls the Paxtons, Toby's parents, and introduces himself as a representative for the law firm of Blaine Morris. He would like to meet with them and discuss a trust settlement in their name. He'll explain it all to them when he arrives. They arrange to meet,Justin and Beth both taking the afternoon off from work.

When they are all seated at the kitchen table, Guy pulls a folder from his briefcase and sets it on the table. "Before I begin, I'd like to say I am so sorry for the loss of your daughter, Penelope."

"Thank you," they both say softly, almost under their breaths.

"As difficult as I am sure this is for you, it's because of her death that I am here today. You are probably familiar with the name Mel Connor."

Justin says, "Of course. The bus driver."

Beth adds quickly, "We don't blame him. We know it was an accident. A terrible accident."

"Yes, it was, but evidently Mel does, or did take the blame and for that reason, he has created a trust fund for your son, Penelope's brother, Toby."

"Oh no, we don't expect to be compensated in any way."

"Evidently, that is no longer possible. You see Mel died recently."

They both look shocked. "Oh no, what happened?"

"We're not quite sure. In addition to representing his lawyer today, I must divulge that I am a detective, investigating the possible murder of both Mel and his wife, Esther. Again, I am so sorry to bring you this awful news."

"What?" Justin stands up quickly, almost knocking his chair over, and starts walking around the kitchen, as if to shake off what he heard.

Beth covers her face with both her hands and starts crying. "I didn't know Mel well, but this is terrible news. And Esther was Toby's fifth-grade teacher. This is awful. When did this happen? Where? I know they moved away but I wasn't sure where they went."

"They moved to Arizona. In a retirement community called Sun Lakes."

"Sun Lakes?" Justin says. He looks at Beth. "Isn't that where your parents are?" He turns to Guy. "Beth's parents rented a house in Arizona recently to spend a few months there. We were there at Christmas. They still have their home in Wichita."

Beth said, "Do my parents know about this?"

Guy says, "I haven't spoken to them. I didn't know they were there. What are their names?"

"Betty and Hank Harrison."

Guy registers a look of surprise, but just nods his head. "I see," he says.

Then it hits him. The text he received from Angelina that he read only after he landed in Wichita. "*Have a safe flight. Let me know when you return. I'm home late afternoon and evening. Only thing on my schedule is lunch with Betty and Hank at their house*."

He stands up and says, "Excuse me. I need to make a quick call." He strides out of the kitchen to the front door and steps onto the front porch.

He hits Angelina's name which is on his favorites list. No answer. Her voice mail comes on. What time is it in Arizona? A little after 1 o'clock. *Pick up Angelina, pick up.*

He leaves a voice mail: "Angelina, if you are still at Betty's leave immediately. Leave now. No questions. Say you feel sick. Anything. Just leave. You may be in danger." He also sends a text with the same message in case she might respond more readily to that.

Then he calls his partner Bill. Voice mail: "Bill, call me as soon as you get this." Then he remembers that Bill is also out of town at his nephew's wedding in New Mexico.

He thinks, *Call Clara. She can go get Angelina.* He doesn't have Clara's number but has Frank's thanks to setting up pickleball matches. Frank answers. *Thank God.*

"Frank, it's Guy. Is Clara there?"

"Right here, chewing me out for forgetting to set the trash out."

"Can I talk to her please. It's important."

"Sure." He hears Frank say, "It's Guy, for you."

He's so happy to hear Clara's voice. "Yes?"

"Clara, don't ask any questions now. I'll explain it all later. Angelina might be in danger. I'm in Kansas and can't reach her. She's having lunch with Betty and Hank Harrison. From pickleball. At their house. Go there. Now. And make her leave with you. Make up any excuse. Say June is sick. Whatever. Call me when you have her out of there. Hurry Clara."

CHAPTER FIFTY-FOUR

Betty says, "I thought we'd have a light lunch. Soup and salad. Nothing too heavy. I tend to get sleepy with a heavy lunch, don't you?"

Angelina smiles and agrees. "Actually, I'm feeling a little sleepy now myself. Makes no sense. I didn't get up early. Maybe I should switch to coffee? Would that be too much trouble?"

"Oh, not at all. Just finish your cocktail and I'll make us a fresh pot of coffee."

Betty gets up and pulls a coffee can out of the cupboard and pours water into the coffeemaker. She sets out three soup bowls and starts to ladle the tortilla soup into them. She sets two off to one side and gives the third one a few drops of something from what looks like an eye-dropper, her back to Angelina, shielding her actions.

When Betty sets the soup bowls at each place setting, Angelina says, "So you're leaving soon. Anxious to get back home? See family I suppose. I bet that cute little girl I saw in her ballet costume."

"Penelope? No, we won't be seeing her. She doesn't live … she's not in Kansas anymore. But we have a grandson, Toby."

Angelina takes a sip of her soup. *Penelope*. An unusual name. Where did she hear that recently? The little girl in the ballet costume photo. But then it hits her. The name on one of Mel's suicide notes that Guy told her about. *Forgive me Penelope.*

Betty says, "Angelina, is your soup okay? Too hot?"

"Oh, no, it's delicious," she says and takes another sip. But she thinks, *Something is not right. I should leave here.* "But you know, I feel so sleepy. I'm so sorry to leave but I think I should since I have to drive home. I really don't know what's wrong with me." She starts to get up.

Betty says, "Oh, I don't think you should drive if you're sleepy. Why don't you stretch out on Hank's recliner? Put your feet up. Just shut your eyes for a few minutes. Maybe that's all it will take And then we'll have that coffee before you drive home."

Angelina stands up but feels wobbly and grips the edge of the table for balance. She thinks she should leave. *Or call Guy. There is something she needs to tell him.* But it's all fuzzy thinking now. *What is it?* She lets Betty lead her to the recliner and she leans into it. She closes her eyes and that feels so good. *Maybe just a few minutes.*

CHAPTER FIFTY-FIVE

Clara and Frank find Betty and Hank's address in the pickleball player list the Fitness Center emailed all the members.

They get into their car and Clara enters the address in their navigation system as Frank pulls out of the driveway. Three miles, it says. Estimated time: six minutes.

"Hurry Frank. Guy said to hurry."

"Now Clara, you know we can't go over 35 miles per hour here. Too many walkers, bikers, golf carts to dodge and go around. We'll get there as soon as we safely can."

Clara says, "I should have driven."

"Oh, sure, and cause a wreck. Settle down woman. Use these six minutes to think about what you're going to say."

When they pull up to Betty and Hank's driveway, they see Angelina's car in the driveway. "Good," Clara says. "It's the right house. You stay in the car. I'll go get her. Don't turn the car off. We may need to make a mad dash out of here."

"We're not robbing a bank, Clara, for heaven's sake. Don't be so dramatic."

Clara jumps out of the car, then runs back. "I better take my phone. Keep yours turned on in case I need help."

"Oh my gosh." Frank shakes his head.

"Oh my gosh, nothing. You weren't the one tied to a chair last time Angelina tried to solve a crime."

"So go," Frank says.

Clara is tempted to barge right in, but rings the doorbell instead. No one responds so she rings it again. This time longer.

Inside the house Betty and Hank are startled at the sound of the doorbell, but Angelina doesn't seem to hear it. She looks peacefully asleep. They look at each other and both shrug their shoulders. Betty mouths a whisper. "Should we answer?"

Hank whispers back. "Let's see if they go away. Give it a minute. Might just be an Amazon package. Sometimes they ring the bell when leave one."

The second long and persistent ring tells them it's not Amazon. Then a loud knocking on the side window panel next to the door. "Hello" says a loud voice from the porch. "Are you home?"

Hank says, "Boy, someone really wants to get our attention. Maybe we should answer. We can send them on their way. We're not doing anything wrong."

They both look at Angelina. "So our guest got sleepy and is taking a little nap. What's the big deal?"

They both approach the front door and when they open it a crack, Clara pushes her way in and almost knocks them over. "Is Angelina here?"

Hank says, "Yes, but she's napping."

"Napping? What are you running here? Senior day care? Where is she?" Clara asks and starts walking past the entry way to the family room. She sees her in the recliner and rushes to her. "Angelina, we have to go. It's June. She's in the hospital. She's asking for you. We need to go now." She starts to pull Angelina out of the chair.

"Just a minute here," Betty says. "Can't you see she's sleeping? Peacefully. We'll take her to the hospital, to this June person, when she wakes up."

"I'll take her now. And maybe not so peacefully. Out of my way, Sister." Clara pushes Betty, who is standing next to the recliner. She starts patting Angelina's cheeks. "Come on honey, get up. Guy said we had to get you out of here."

At the mention of Guy's name Betty and Hank freeze and look at one another.

Betty says, "I thought it was June who needs Angelina. Now you're changing your story?

Who are you anyway?"

"I'm Clara. Anyway. Angelina's friend and June's friend. And Guy told me June needs Angelina."

They are so into each other's faces, that they don't notice that Angelina has opened her eyes. She starts to speak, words slightly slurred. "Clara, what …?"

"Thank goodness you're awake. You have to come with me now. June needs you. She's in the hospital."

"Hospital?" Angelina says softly and looks confused.

"Later, we'll explain later. Can you stand up?" She tries to help Angelina out of the chair. "What did you guys do to her? Slip her a mickey?" She turns around and sees the kitchen table with three place settings. Only one place has a martini glass with some liquid still in it. "I don't know what's going on here, but we're out of here."

Clara, at five-feet-ten inches, practically lifts five-foot Angelina into her arms and drags her out the front door.

CHAPTER FIFTY-SIX

Hank seems stunned but Betty goes into action immediately. She dumps the rest of the drink from the martini glass as well as the pitcher that contained more of the "cocktail" down the drain. She rinses both of them out. She throws out Angelina's bowl of soup and throws the eye dropper into a plastic baggie. She digs into a drawer and pulls out a small mallet she uses as a meat tenderizer. She pounds the plastic bag, shredding the contents to pieces.

"I'll throw this in the neighbor's trash when we leave."

"Where are we going?" Hank asks.

Betty says, "Time to get out of Dodge. Now. Quick. We better load up our car and head out."

Betty looks out the window. "Oh no, Angelina's car is behind ours."

Hank smiles and pulls Angelina's key fob from his pocket. He dangles them proudly.

Betty yells, "Thank God for that. Hurry Hank. Take what you need. I doubt we'll ever be back."

She runs into the bedroom "Where's your phone? We need to destroy both of ours. They can track us that way." Hank looks bewildered and just stands there.

Betty screams at him. "Hank, hurry. We've got to get to the bank and withdraw all our cash. We'll need it. And somewhere along the way, we might need to ditch this car. Or take a bus. Can't leave a trail."

CHAPTER FIFTY-SEVEN

Frank sees Clara coming out of the house practically carrying Angelina. He rushes to help. "What in the …," he asks.

Clara almost shouts, "Talk later. Help me get her in the car."

Together they manage to slide her across the back seat where she closes her eyes again.

"Isn't that her car?" Frank asks.

"Oh my gosh, we've got to get her purse and keys."

Clara runs back in the house, shouting to Betty who is pounding something on the counter and doesn't seem to hear her. "I need Angelina's purse," Clara shouts. Then she spots it on the foyer table with a scarf draped across it. She grabs it and runs back to her car. She starts digging through it for keys. Frustrated, she dumps the entire contents on her lap. No keys.

"Frank, call Guy. Tell him we have her."

Frank says, "Guy's on speaker phone."

Guy's voice is frantic. "Thank goodness you got there. Is she alright?"

"Not sure. Opened her eyes once but keeps falling asleep."

"Get her to the emergency room. Quick. Pump her stomach. Hurry."

Clara says, "We can't waste time now for her car. We'll come back."

CHAPTER FIFTY-EIGHT

Once they pump Angelina's stomach and start an IV to restore fluids, she seems to be resting comfortably but they keep her overnight. Clara and Frank stay with her until visiting hours are over and know that Guy is on the way home.

From the airport he calls the precinct and advises them of the situation, saying "Get someone to the Harrison home and bring them in for questioning."

Guy arrives at the hospital a few hours later, long after visiting hours, but uses his detective ID and badge to get past the nurse's station and into Angelina's room. She appears to be sleeping so he doesn't want to disturb her. He simply takes her hand resting on her blanket nearest to him and holds it, rubbing his hand over and over it gently.

She opens her eyes. "Guy," she says, "You're here."

"And you're here." he says, "That's what's most important. You're still here, among the living." Then takes her hand and puts it to his lips with a soft kiss.

"What in the world …," she starts to ask, but he puts a finger to her lips and says, "Shhhhh. We have plenty of time to talk later. Just rest now and I'll be back in the morning to take you home if they release you. I just had to see that you were alright."

"I am now," she says as she squeezes his hand.

Then she opens her eyes half-way. "I heard they pumped my stomach. Do you think I lost any weight?" She closes her eyes as she drifts off to sleep.

CHAPTER FIFTY-NINE

Guy and Angelina are home now, and he fills her in.

"We found prescription bottles with liquid in the medicine cabinet. My guess is that the lab will show it is Nembutal. And at first glance, the text on those notes looks to be from a typewriter. We got a warrant for a search of the Wichita house and they came up with an old IBM Selectric. They'll also test for fingerprints to confirm."

Angelina says, "They must have been in a big hurry to get away to leave the obvious evidence of a poisonous substance. How will you find them now? They could be anywhere. Miles away."

"Oh, we'll find them. They'll mess up somewhere along the way. Amateurs that they are. Not professional killers. Today's technology tracking is smarter than most criminals."

When Guy and Angelina talk, as relieved as they are that she escaped bodily harm, they express little joy. Rather their conversation is a somber one.

"I can't imagine losing a grandchild. It's a horrendous loss." Angelina dabs her eyes with a tissue.

"Revenge is a strong motive. It must have festered until it was out of control." Guy says.

"And so sad that the love they had for Penelope somehow led to such hatred."

"Crimes of passion often stem from love." Guy says. "Love lost, love denied. It seems the deeper the love, the greater the loss."

Angelina says, "So sad for their daughter. Losing her child and now maybe never seeing her parents again. Now it's like Toby has lost his grandparents too. They'll never get to see him or enjoy his life."

"They'll find a way to see him and that's how we will find them. It may take a while but it will happen. Be assured."

"Do you think the daughter will cooperate with the law or protect her parents if they reach out?" Angelina asks.

"That's a tough call and only time will tell. There's Toby to consider. If they aid and abet a criminal, they could face charges and jail time. Somewhere the vicious cycle has to stop."

Then Guy adds, "The most puzzling aspect of all this is why they killed Esther first. She wasn't driving the bus. I guess possibly to throw us off as to motive."

"Oh, I think I know why." Angelina says.

"Really? Miss Marple. Tell me your theory. Can't wait to hear this."

"It's rather obvious I think." Angelina waits a minute before continuing as if she wants to keep Guy in suspense. "Killing Mel was too painless a punishment for him. According to the notes they sent, I think they wanted him to suffer first. To suffer the loss of a loved one like they did."

"Ah, you are so perceptive. There is that twist that you told me to look for. And which Agatha Christie novel gave you that insight?"

"What? You're giving Agatha credit for my intuitiveness?"

"Pardon me. *Grosso error. Big mistake.* Of course, it was all you." He spreads his arms out as if to acknowledge it.

"I forgive you." Angelina says as she goes into his widespread arms. "I guess this whole tragedy is really about forgiveness, isn't it?"

Guy says, "Or lack of. Some people can forgive the worst of transgressions while others cling to the slightest infraction. A human mystery."

"I actually had this discussion with Clara and June. Clara, of course, was out for blood. Catch them and make them pay for their horrendous deeds. Said she never got picked for jury duty because she answered every question with 'Just hang the bastard.'

June, on the other hand, said, 'It's simply grace. To forgive is a special grace. Grace exists in acts of forgiveness. If we are so blessed with it, we can't help but live our lives in peace and harmony.'"

"Wow, I think you just gave a powerful sermon there," Guy says.

"Oh, not me. That's our Junie, who then shared all the Gummy bears in her purse with us."

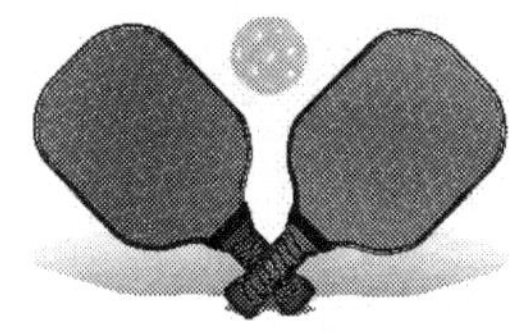

The next time Angelina, Clara, and June play Scrabble they ponder.

Clara says, "I hope this board game doesn't prove to be as dangerous as our past activities. Myra dies in Mah Jonng, Esther dies in pickleball. Maybe we should be playing Clue."

June says, "No, Angelina would win every time. She's too good at solving murders."

Clara says, "Okay, badminton anyone?"

June says, "Too physical. How about Chutes and Ladders?"

BLEACHER CHATTER

SOMEWHERE IN FLORIDA

"Looks like we got a new couple on the courts. They seem like decent players. Always good to have some new blood."

"Sure is. I'm tired of looking at your wrinkly old face across the net," one guy says as he slaps the other one on the back.

"Hey, I resemble that remark."

"Anybody know their names or where they're from?"

"No, they kind of keep to themselves. Don't seem to want to socialize much. We invited them to the mixer after Saturday night play but they declined."

"I'd like to know where she got that fancy water bottle cover. I think that's hers." He points to a bag hanging on the fence with a water bottle in the side pockets, sticking out enough to see all the bling-bling on it.

EPILOGUE

The large paper map of the 50 states is unfolded and spread out on Angelina's dining room table with a yellow legal pad, a swatch of sticky notes and magic markers beside it. A tiny red and white box of gold foil stars is open and Guy is placing them at various spots on the map.

He says, "I think we start here," he places one gold star close to the Arizona-Mexico border. "And then we circle back and head west." He refers to his tablet and makes a check beside number one on the legal pad. Tubac.

"Do you really think we will get to every one of those restaurants?" Angelina shakes her head in wonderment.

"This summer the West and if it goes well and we want to do it again, we'll go east in the fall. Lobster, clam chowder, and the beautiful fall colors. And of course a stop in Chicago for deep dish pizza."

"And all your relatives, who I can't wait to meet. Especially your sisters."

"I'm calling for our first room reservation right now." He refers to the number beside Tubac on the yellow pad and punches in the numbers.

Angelina hears him saying, "Yes, I'd like to reserve a casita for two nights, starting next Friday." Pause. " Just a minute, let me check." He looks to Angelina. "Two rooms? One room double beds?" Then he gives her a pleading look, "Or one room, one bed?"

Angelina says, "I think it's time for one room, one bed." She walks toward him and he puts his arm around her as he completes the call.

His huge and tender smile tells her she made the right decision. She reaches up and strokes the stubble she has come to love on his Italian cheek.

She says, "I thought you'd never ask. I've had my overnight bag with the pretty pink lounge wear packed for months."

THE END

Discover how Guy and Angelina first meet as they solve the mysterious death of a friend and Mah Jongg player in the foursome which includes ditzy June and sensible Clara.

A MAH JONGG MYSTERY

Chapter One

When Angelina hears that they found Myra's dead body naked in the shower with the water still running, she immediately suspects foul play. Knowing Myra was frugal—one might even say a penny pincher—Angelina believes Myra would have turned off the water even if it was the last thing she did.

Now as she stands beside Myra's graveside, her thoughts drift as the minister drones on. This isn't her first funeral and won't be her last as her friends are aging, yet each death causes her to evaluate and judge her entire existence.

Will I have regrets on my deathbed for things not done? What about my bucket list? Will I have time to make amends with those I've offended? Yes, death definitely makes one examine one's life.

A cactus wren chirps cheerily, oblivious to sadness as it flits from tree to tree. Orange blossoms emit wafts of sweet citrus fragrance. Springtime is in bloom in the Phoenix desert with the ocotillos' fiery russet buds and the Saguaro cactus sprouting pink floral trumpets. So many reminders of new life, but while the crocus is pushing up, Myra is pushing down. Six feet down.

Myra's three daughters stand together in somber dresses, holding hands. Angelina thinks of her daughter, April, and feels the familiar pang of regret for how her relationship with her has crumbled. Myra's sudden death reminds her that life is precarious.

Behind Myra's daughters stand the grandchildren with their dads. One of the sons-in-law keeps looking at his watch. It's Debbie's husband, the dentist. *Does he have an urgent root canal waiting or what?*

Beside Angelina, June sniffs in her handkerchief, while Clara stands stoic with head lowered. Even their shoes reflect their personalities. Clara is wearing sensible Oxfords. June has cutesy, open-toed heels that will, in spite of her petite stature, sink into the moist sod with each step she takes. Eccentricities and all, Angelina is glad to have them beside her now and grateful for their friendship. She is also reminded that with Myra gone, their Mah Jongg foursome is reduced to three.

Like the cactus wren's flight, her thoughts flit from one thing to another. What really caused Myra's death? Angelina has read enough whodunits to know that the unattended death of a healthy woman is labeled suspicious and requires a police investigation, but maybe she should also do a little sleuthing herself. This is after all just like page one of the mysteries she devours—a sudden death, a funeral scene, a curious friend with a vivid imagination.

A wayward thought strikes her. Another irony. Today is Monday. Myra said it was her favorite day for the 3 M's. Mah Jongg Mavens at Myra's."

Is it possible there is a fourth M in Myra's life? M as in murder?

Violetta Armour lives in Sun Lakes, Arizona, where she enjoys the active lifestyle her retirement community offers. Former careers include book store ownership, a Dale Carnegie instructor, an English teacher and University of Phoenix instructor. Her current passions are playing pickleball, visiting book clubs who select her books, walking her Covid rescue dog, Lola, and spoiling her grandchildren. Her debut novel, I'll Always Be With You has won awards, followed by the sequel, Still With You. A Mah Jongg Mystery and S'mores Can Be Deadly are the first two books in her Dangerous Pastime Series. And she makes good lasagna.

Made in the USA
Columbia, SC
08 October 2021